North of Dog Island

The characters and events in this book are fictional and
any resemblance to actual persons or events is coincidental.

ISBN: 1-4392-6120-2
ISBN-13: 9781439261200
Library of Congress Control Number: 2009911282

North of Dog Island

Aaron A. Lehman

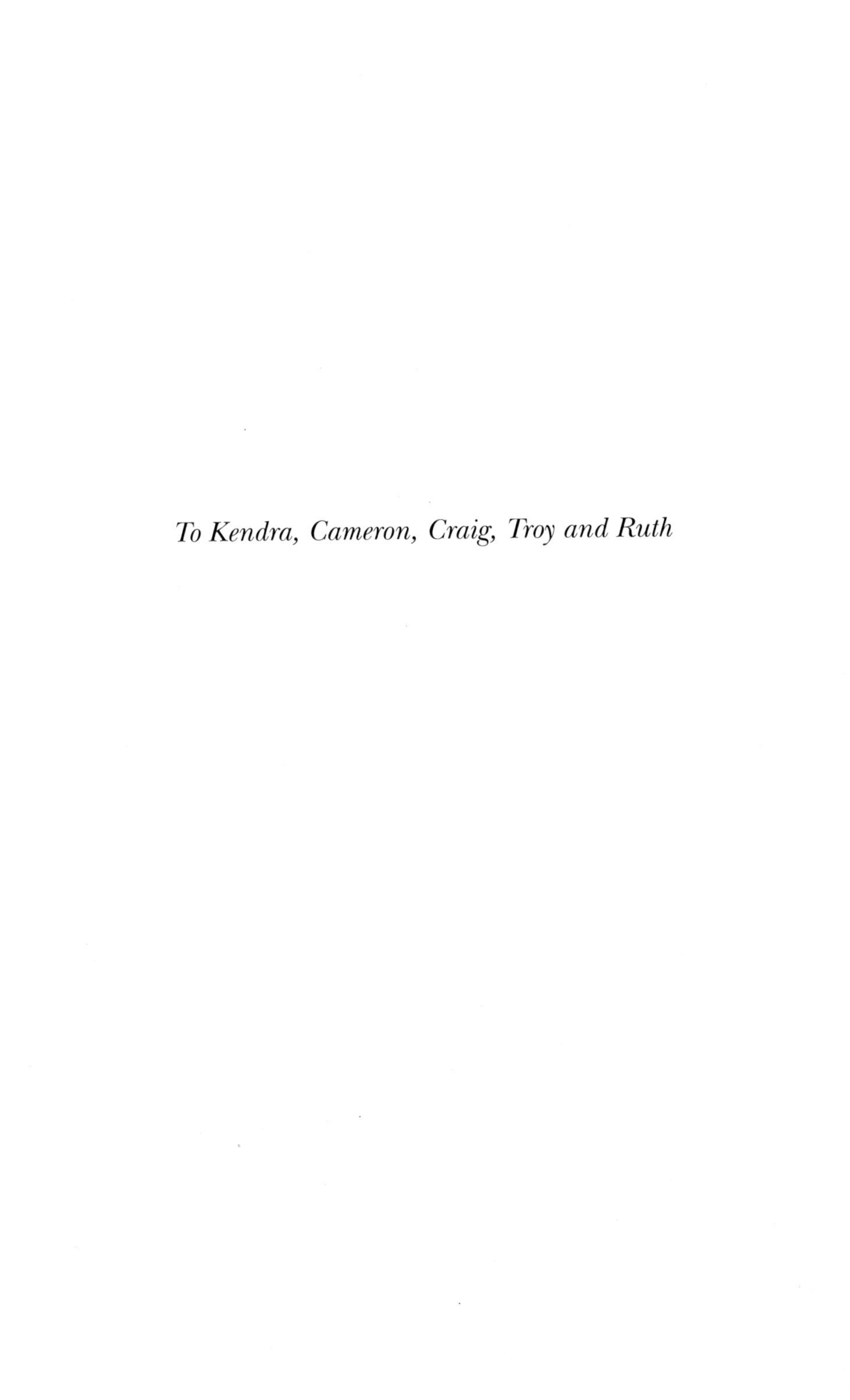

To Kendra, Cameron, Craig, Troy and Ruth

ACKNOWLEDGEMENTS:

Pauline Auger–Alberta Education Aboriginal Curriculum Consultant

Wayne Bowles–Forest Fire Inspector

Yvonne Chartrand–Métis Dancing

Jamie Coutts–Lesser Slave Regional Fire Service

*Chief Roy DeLaRonde–Traditional Status Métis Paddle Wedding Ceremony–
All efforts to make contact have failed. To allow permission to cite in subsequent printings, please contact Aaron A. Lehman.

Keith Denoncourt–Alberta Conservation Education Teacher and Consultant

Gina Donald–Métis Dancing

Helen Gall–Sketches

Kelly Harlton–Wildside Wilderness Connection

HOLY BIBLE – NEW INTERNATIONAL VERSION – Zondervan Bible Publishers

Terry Jessiman – Alberta Sustainable Resource Development

MJ Munn-Kristoff – Lesser Slave Forest Education

Winifred Lehman – Editing

Margaret Loney – Aboriginal Awareness Instructor

Linda McCauley – Métis Dancing

Mark Missal – Missal Enterprises-Air Attack Services

Trudie Moon – Computer

Terry Mosher – Editing

Kylie Sais – Norman Chief Memorial Square Dancers

CHAPTER 1

Sandy Lake, north of Slave Lake and Dog Island, remains etched in the minds of all who venture north to visit this somewhat rounded lake with its beautiful sandy beaches. Not a large lake, it is large enough to support a commercial and recreational fishery, its shores, with a cover of trees and shrubs are always visible in the distance. Its south shore is home to a number of Métis families, some who still live by the old ways. The forest industry and oil and gas exploration are making inroads into this once isolated and pristine lake, but the north shore is still isolated and it provides a living for the few trappers who wish to pursue the lifestyle, for this allows them to remain intimately connected with the land which can sustain them, as it has provided for their ancestors for centuries.

Raymond and his wife, Arlene, with their young daughter, Sylvia, decided to move here from Slave Lake to live by the old ways, taking over a trap line from a distant relative, Uncle Henry, who was getting too old to work it and who needed to be closer to his family in Sandy Lake. Raymond, a tall, strong, muscular, dark-haired nehiyaw, as the Cree refer to themselves, who had apprenticed as a mechanic in Slave Lake, was now self-assured in his ways and he was in control of his world. Raymond had learned the old ways from his kohkom, her Elder friends and from Uncle Henry, who taught him how to run the trap line. Arlene, a fiery, strong-headed Métis woman with gorgeous, long, red hair, had taken Early Childhood and Native Arts courses at Northern Lakes College in Slave Lake. She had the tenacity and strength to help Raymond on the trap line, yet the soft-hearted touch to be a great mother to Sylvia and a loving companion to Raymond. Sylvia, a typical three year old girl, had the dark hair and brown eyes of Raymond and the strong will and tenacity of Arlene. Fresh into the world, she anxiously explored any and all of the exciting things and events of her new environment.

On this bright, sunny, spring morning, Raymond and Arlene were in the process of tanning a moose hide, the animal having provided them with their winter supply of meat. As the cool of the morning faded, the warmth of the day brought a slight breeze from the shimmering surface of the lake, with its mixture of blue, violet, red and yellow hues. The geese, ducks and other water birds were claiming their nesting sites. The male songbirds, back from their wintering grounds, were producing a mixture of warbling songs, each trying to establish a territory and to attract a mate. Some were already flying over and around the small, but solid, snug, trapper's cabin with nesting materials in their bills. Raymond and Arlene were building a new and larger cabin, hoping to have it ready by next winter.

Raymond hunched over the moose hide, scraping at the fat and bloody tissue still on the hide that was stretched across a pole frame. The scraper, fashioned from a leg bone of a moose, had a strap that looped around Raymond's arm, to provide him with extra leverage while scraping. Over and over, he scraped from top to bottom, hard enough to remove the fat, but not so hard that he would damage the hide. He made sure he did what Kohkom and the Elders had taught him.

Arlene was around the corner of the cabin. She had prepared the moose brain mixture which would be used in the tanning process and she was preparing a proper fire pit next to a pile of heavily rotted black spruce stumps which would provide the smoke necessary for smoking the hide when the scraping and tanning was finished. It took a lot of work to scrape, to tan and to smoke a hide, to produce soft leather, useful for making moccasins and other leather products.

"Hey, Arlene," Raymond called. "There's something wrong with this picture. Aren't the women folk supposed to be slaving over the moose hide, while the men relax around the smoking fire?"

"We're in this together. Remember?" Arlene retorted, as she peered around the corner through the smoke.

Raymond groaned as he made a final scrape with the moose leg scraper, and he gave a sigh as he wiped the sweat from his forehead. The smells of the fat and blood, mixed with his body odour, were starting to give him a headache.

"I think I like car grease on my hands better than this stuff."

As Raymond climbed off the stretched hide, he looked around.

"Sylvia?"

Noticing that Sylvia was gone, Raymond called, "Arlene!"

"Arlene, is Sylvia with you?"

"No. I thought she was with you."

"She was right here! Now she's not!"

"Sylvia," Raymond called.

"Sylvia," Arlene called.

"Sylvia! Sylvia-a-a-a!"

Their voices were caught up in the gusts of wind that were coming from a new direction. No longer were there soft breezes coming from the lake. Strong harsh winds were blowing in from the southeast, bearing ugly, black clouds, threatening a major storm. In spite of his turmoil, Raymond remembered an earlier time.

• • •

CHAPTER 2

An earlier time

A small crowd gathered around Marg's cabin. Decorations streamed from the cabin and the smoke house. Old people, young people and small children were all mingling with one another. Raymond and Arlene, Jack and Susan, Allen and Rose, Larry and Emily, Arlene's parents, Kohkom and the Elders, along with the local priest were all sporting some type of traditional dress and were in a festive mood. The occasion was the wedding of Raymond and Arlene. Raymond was not one for pomp and ceremony, but Arlene insisted on a traditional Métis Paddle Wedding.

Yes, this was Raymond and Arlene, the high school Arlene who had caused Raymond so much grief by teasing and embarrassing him. Yes, this was the Arlene who came looking for him on Dog Island on a seadoo with Susan. Yes, this was the same Arlene and her friend Susan, whom Raymond had rescued from a dog attack. Yes, this was the Raymond who had noticed that, without the braces on her teeth, Arlene was a pretty redhead. He was attracted, not only by her looks, but also by her spirited manner, her sense of humour and her outlook on life. Arlene always knew she wanted Raymond to be her Indian Warrior, but she had to take the indirect, more subtle route to her goal. On the seadoo, returning from Dog Island with Raymond's arms wrapped tightly around her body, she knew she had trapped him.

The couple and their attendants were attentive to the words of the priest. Arlene and Raymond stood side-by-side in their wedding apparel. Arlene had a traditional dress with intricate stitching and bead work. Raymond's vest, over his white shirt, had matching beadwork. Jewelry, designed and made by Arlene, adorned the neck and hands of both the bride and groom. The bride held a beautiful bouquet of locally grown and collected flowers. The groom wore a red, woven sash around his waist, with the tails hanging down on one side. The smiles of the couple lit up the ceremony, as the rays of sunshine showered the crowd with gleams and sparkles from the diamond rings.

The priest began to read:

"Love is patient,

love is kind.

It does not envy, it does not boast, it is not proud.

It is not rude, it is not self-seeking, it is not easily angered,

It keeps no record of wrongs.

Love does not delight in evil but rejoices with the truth.

It always protects, always trusts, always hopes,

always perseveres."

A local Elder proceeded with the Traditional Métis Paddle Wedding ceremony.

"To the Great Spirits of the East, South, West and North, we give thanks to the Creator, of all things. Much of our heritage and our culture involves the traps, snowshoes, axe, canoe and paddles. There are two paddles over you now, (pointing to the two paddles the attendants held crisscrossed over their heads), but I am going to take them from you and to replace them with one paddle.

The one paddle represents your coming together as one. No more me, me, just we, we and ours. The paddle represents a smooth voyage together, but you know every day will not be smooth. When the water gets rough, you have to paddle a little harder. Sometimes you have to put ashore, make a campfire and use your paddle as a fan to get your fire going. The same is true in everyday life. Look to the Great Spirit for guidance, fan the flame of your love and don't let silence come between you. There should always be laughter and discussions."*

The couple was then declared husband and wife and the official papers were signed. Congratulations were offered to the couple, first from the parents and then by the rest of the guests. According to tradition, everyone brought food and gifts for the wedding feast.

"I don't believe this," Jack said, as he congratulated the couple. "Raymond, you've found your Indian Princess and Arlene, you've found your Indian Warrior. Congratulations. I am really happy for you both. Keep in touch."

"Tânsi, Raymond ekwa, Arlene," Marg, Raymond's kohkom said, as she timidly approached the newly wed couple. "Long ago, girls were married young and the man was chosen by the parents. If a young man accepted a bowl of soup from his future bride and she accepted a pair of moccasins from him, a marriage contract was made. Sometimes he had to pay, maybe a horse or something. The wedding was usually in the winter and it could last for days. The bride was taken to her new home, bundled up in a dog sled."

"Wow!" Arlene said. "I'm glad things have changed."

"Here's a little something for both of you. I hope they warm your hearts as well as your feet." She pulled out two pairs of beautifully beaded mukluks.

"These are beautiful!" Arlene exclaimed. "Thank you so much." They both gave her a big hug.

The mukluks were made of smoke tanned moose hide and there were matching floral designs on the top of each foot and a beaded cuff on the high top. There was satin binding, beaded edging and silk tassels hanging down the front. The pleasant smell of tanning smoke filled the air.

"There is a story here," Kohkom said, pointing to the bead work. "These flower patterns tell about the life of plants. See the stems, leaves, buds, flowers, pollen, seed pods and seeds?" as she pointed to each one.

"Wow, this is the life cycle of plants!" Raymond exclaimed. He hadn't realized Kohkom knew her biology. Maybe she did know what she was talking about when she told her stories.

Kohkom continued. "You can see the seed pods on the cuff dropping the seeds. Some have landed on the top of the boot around the flower. They make the new plants. Life continues. Just like you and Arlene. Now you will give our life and culture to your young ones."

"Here. Try these on. They will be great for dancing the jig," Kohkom said, with a teary twinkle in her eye. She knew Raymond was going to have a hard time jigging when the celebration started.

"Let the music begin!" someone called out.

• • •

CHAPTER 3

"Come on, Raymond. Let's dance," Arlene said as she pulled him up and over to the area that had been prepared for the wedding dance. "Hey, put your sash on the left side now. You're taken."

Red, white and blue colours in the sash represented Métis flags. Black told of the dark times in history and green was for the plants and herbs. Yellow honoured the wearer and the side it was worn indicated his status.

Raymond and Arlene and the others danced the slow waltzes. Later, Raymond danced with Arlene's mother as Arlene danced with Allen. Everyone was having a good time; then, Arlene gave a nod to the band leader and all at once, the band cut into the fast toe tapping music and fancy footwork of the Red River Jig.

"What are you doing?" Raymond yelled, as Arlene took off on the intricate steps and heel to toe movements of the single toe, double step, around the horn and other common jig steps.

"Come on! Let's jig." Raymond was left behind as others joined Arlene. The music reached a crescendo of fiddle music, accompanied by guitar and bass and the foot work of traditional dancers. The bows, twirls and spins of a square dance finished the first round of dancing.

Completely exhausted and out of breath, Arlene slumped beside Raymond. "You don't know how to jig?" Arlene asked.

"No," Raymond replied with a bit of sarcasm. "I do Indian dancing, not this fiddle stuff," he said with a smile.

"Well, this is Indian music too. You'd better learn to like it. Come on. I'll teach you to jig."

The most famous Métis dance is the Red River Jig. The accompanying fiddle tune is sometimes called the Métis anthem, with the fiddle having the G string, tuned to an A, making a unique sound. The fiddler uses a small section of the bow to give short bursts of music in 2/4 time and he keeps the rhythm going with both feet. The jig was very popular in the mid-1800s and it was known throughout the North Country, where the Métis lived along the major waterways and where they traveled onto the prairies for the buffalo hunt. Red River carts, drawn by oxen or horse, moved families from one camp to another. Jigging is a combination of First Nation's footwork and Scottish, Irish and French-Canadian dance forms. The basic jig step, or circle step of the high sound is still danced in most Métis communities, with local dancers adding their own fancy steps or changes during the low segments of the tune.

"Come on," Arlene encouraged Raymond. "Put your foot like this. Then step back four times, then front step four times and triple tap four times like this."

Raymond was still back-stepping when Arlene was already tapping. What a mix up! Arlene soon joined the others and she was jigging the mother of all jigs. Raymond was a bit despondent as others joined Arlene for a number of jigs, reels and square dances. Some had interesting names such as "Whiskey before Breakfast" and "Reel of Eight".

There are different theories as to how the Red River Jig originated, but one says that the tune came about at a wedding in 1860 when a Mr. Macdallas composed a new fiddle tune for the celebration. Father Boucher, the officiating priest, called it the Red River Jig. Over the years, other steps have been added to the basic steps, such as the Jumping Jack, Bunny Step and the Heel Step. There are now over one hundred different fancy steps.

Other people came by and they tried to help Raymond learn the new dance. He wasn't exactly a klutz, but he could relate better to the steady beat of the bass than he could to the fast, "all-over-the-place" tune of the fiddle.

A young boy, with spiked hair, came up to Raymond and said, "Follow me. Put one foot here, the other foot there. Just shake your bum lots and scream. No one will ever notice how you dance."

Arlene came back and started shaking her bum next to Raymond's. The kid took off.

"It will take a little practice," Arlene said, "but, some day, you will be a good jigging partner. I'll teach you the Drop of Brandy and the Duck Dance."

"That's what we were doing."

"Yeah, right!"

Suddenly, Raymond grabbed Arlene and swept her off her feet. He twirled and spun her round and round. In his dizziness, Raymond reached back to the basic beat of the drums common to his culture. He heard and felt the spirited jigging of Arlene's culture and he watched as they blended together in front of him. They held each other tightly and they shared a prolonged kiss.

"I may not be a voyageur," Raymond said, "but I'm ready to take this voyage with you."

"We only have one paddle. Remember?" Arlene retorted, as they hugged each other, laughed and tried to stop the spinning in their heads.

"Pe mîcisok," someone called in Cree. "Come and eat. The feast is ready."

"Let's go," Arlene said, as she grabbed Raymond's arm to help him up.

"I'm not hungry."

Arlene gave him a surprised look.

Raymond jumped to his feet, picked her up and started running.

"I'm always hungry!"

• • •

CHAPTER 4

Raymond worked at a local garage as an apprentice mechanic and he enjoyed his work. He loved the feel of grease on his hands and the smell of engines being repaired. He also loved fixing things for his customers, making them and his boss happy. If other mechanics were having trouble recognizing a problem, Raymond seemed to be able to diagnose the cause and to give advice about fixing it.

"Hey, Raymond," Chris called. "What is wrong with this light? I can't find the problem."

"It's probably a computer problem. Hook up to the scanner and see what it says."

"What do you think you're doing?" Jeff asked when he saw Raymond using a stethoscope on the engine of the car he was working on. "Do you think that engine has a heart?" he taunted.

"Sometimes, you can tell what is wrong by listening to an engine when it is running. A stethoscope makes the sound louder and easier to tell what is wrong."

"Here. Let me check your engine," Raymond said, as he grabbed Jeff and tried to listen to his heart. "Maybe we'll check your blood pressure as well."

• • •

Raymond loved his job; he loved Arlene and he loved living in Old Town, Slave Lake, originally know as Sawridge. They didn't need a fancy place and they were happy when Kohkom suggested they move a mobile home onto part of her place in Old Town. Raymond was close to the river and the oxbow and he could pop in on Kohkom to see how she was doing and, of course, he could sample her moose meat and bannock to see if she could still cook.

"Maybe you're getting too old to be a good kohkom," Raymond teased on one of his recent visits. "It is my duty, as a good nôsisim (grandson) to check out your cooking every now and then to see if it's still okay to eat."

"I could cook you fish guts and you'd still think it was great," Kohkom teased back. They both laughed.

"Who's cooking fish guts?" Arlene chortled as she burst into the cabin. I'll bet Kohkom's cooking is better than yours any day."

"You're right," Raymond said. "Even when I cook moose meat, it ends up tasting like tofu."

"Why don't you two stay and eat with me? I'll put on another piece of moose meat. Here, Arlene, you bake the bannock. Raymond probably forgot how."

"Okay, okay. You two women are ganging up on me," Raymond retorted.

The banter and laughter continued throughout the evening.

"The Native Arts class I'm taking at the college is going to show us how to tan a moose hide the old way," Arlene related. "They are looking for a place to put up a frame to stretch the hide. I'm thinking there might be a place out here that we could use to tan it."

"There is a lot of space over by the oxbow and a lot of rotten wood to make the smoke," Marg told her.

"I could tend the fire, as the men did in the olden days," Raymond said, laughing. "Tanning is women's work."

"Yeah, right," Arlene responded. "Well, this is the modern age and you always said you wanted to learn the old ways."

"That's right," Marg said. "I can tend the fire and you can put your big muscles to work doing something useful, instead of rubbing that car grease on your hands to make everyone think you actually work over at that garage."

"Well," Raymond said, "you are both right, as usual. It would be great to have everybody out here working on tanning a hide. I'd be glad to help."

"They said anyone could help if they wanted to. I'll let the teachers know."

"Thanks for the food," Raymond called as he and Arlene headed out the door. "You're still a good kohkom."

On the way home, Raymond reminded Arlene of some news she didn't want to hear.

"The boss said arrangements have been made for me to go to school in the city. It is a six weeks' course and part of my training as a mechanic."

"I know, but I don't want you to go. Can't you just go to the college here?"

"No, they don't offer a program for mechanics."

"Well, I don't like it. Where are you going to stay?"

"My friend Jack is in Edmonton and he said I could bunk in with him. I can come home with him on the weekends."

"Well, I don't like it!" she yelled as she ran for the oxbow.

"I know," he said as he chased after her.

They stood for a long time hugging each other as the moonlight glistened off cheeks wet with streams of tears.

• • •

CHAPTER 5

Raymond arrived home from Edmonton, having completed his first six week apprenticeship course. He and Arlene had been celebrating his return with soup and bannock at Kohkom's cabin. The mood was jovial, with Raymond teasing Marg about her cooking. Arlene was rather subdued and in a pensive mood. She wasn't sure when to break the good news. Should she tell Raymond when they were alone or should she include Marg when making the announcement? Would Raymond take it as good news?

"We are going to have a baby," Arlene finally said in a quiet voice.

"Miywâsin!" Kokhom laughed. I'm so happy for you. We need awâsisak around here. There are way too many old people now."

Raymond sat stunned. He didn't know how to react.

Arlene reached out, hugged him and repeated. "We're going to have a baby. You are going to be a father."

"But I don't know how to be a father," Raymond protested.

"You'll learn," Arlene assured him.

"You'll have some time to get used to the idea. It'll take awhile, but you'll like it. Trust me," Marg said.

"I know how to change an engine, but I have no idea how to change a diaper."

"We'll put a clothes pin on your nose and you won't know the difference," Arlene chuckled. She was feeling better already. Raymond would make a great father.

"Hey, you're already a great kohkom," Raymond teased Marg. "Now, you'll be a great grand kohkom (anisko câpân). Maybe it will improve your cookin."

Marg came over and gave them both a big hug.

• • •

Time passed quickly. Even though Raymond was a mechanic, he was also a pretty good carpenter. He was going to be a father and he insisted on getting everything ready for the little one. He started building a small bed in the spare room of the mobile home. He and Arlene enjoyed planning for the new arrival. They did renovating, painting, and decorating. They didn't want to know if they were going to have a boy or a girl. They wanted to be surprised. Of course, Raymond was hoping for a little warrior.

"How about painting one wall blue and the other one pink since we don't know if we are having a boy or a girl," Raymond teased Arlene.

"No way. You stick to carpentry and I'll do the painting," she replied.

"How about orange?"

"Get out of here," Arlene said as she ushered Raymond out of the room. "It's going to be pink."

"How do you know we're having a girl?"

"Kohkom told me."

"How does she know?"

"Ancient kohkom secret."

"Yah, right!"

• • •

Months passed and Raymond felt in control, at the centre of his world.

One day, while Raymond was working on a pickup truck, he answered the telephone and it felt as if his heart had jumped into his throat. He dropped his wrench and he accidentally kicked over a can of oil.

"I've had a baby!" Raymond shouted over the noise of the shop.

"Wow, I think you've been breathing too much exhaust," Jim chided. "I didn't even know you were pregnant," he laughed.

"That was Arlene's Mom. She took Arlene to the hospital and we have a baby. She wasn't due yet, but I guess the little warrior wanted to get out to take on the world."

"Is it a boy?"

"She didn't even say."

"Let us know when you deliver!" Jim yelled, as Raymond was running for the truck, his coveralls half off and dragging on the ground.

Raymond was scared as he entered the hospital. Everything was strange. He had never needed the hospital before. He had just used the clinic whenever he needed to see a doctor. He knew his way around a machine shop, but the human shop scared him. Here was where they took people apart and there was blood and pain.

"I have a new baby," Raymond stuttered to the nurse at the desk.

"You must be Raymond," the nurse said in a friendly voice. "Everyone is waiting for you. Follow me."

Shyly, Raymond entered the room.

"Raymond," Arlene said with tears of joy in her eyes. This is our little girl."

Raymond was stunned, trying to hold back the tears. Maybe he had been breathing too much exhaust. He was becoming a mushy woose, but this little bundle, with a round face and black hair, caused his tears to flow.

Finally, Raymond composed himself and he said softly, with a twinkle in his eye, "I thought you said we were going to have a boy."

"Raymond," Arlene said, trying to show some exasperation, "Kohkom said we were going to have a girl. See, she was right."

"Well, she looks like a little girl warrior," Raymond said, as Arlene held up the baby for Raymond to see. He was overwhelmed. All he could do was give a gentle hug to both of his girls.

"What should we name her?" Arlene asked.

"Hey, wait a minute. Things are going way too fast. I want to know how you had this baby so fast."

"Well, I thought I was just having false labour, but I called my Mom anyway. She brought me to the hospital and these nice people told me it was for real. They all helped me deliver this little miracle."

"You were a real pain," Arlene said as she snuggled the baby.

"You have a very brave woman," one nurse said to Raymond. "She did really well for the first baby. It usually takes a long, hard labour for the first one, but she didn't take long at all."

"We need to thank all of these people for making this a special time," Raymond said.

"So, what is the name?" a nurse asked.

"My grandmother's name is Sylvia. How do you like that, Raymond?"

"I love it, and both of you."

Raymond was awestruck as Arlene handed the little bundle of moving arms and legs to him. He was afraid to handle her. He knew how to work a wrench, but this was totally different.

"I can't wait to show Sylvia to my folks and to Kohkom. This is awesome!"

• • •

CHAPTER 6

On a cool autumn day, when Raymond came home from the garage, he could hardly find a parking spot around his place. There were cars and trucks everywhere.

"What is going on around here?" he asked Arlene as she ran up to his truck.

"One of the Native Arts' students just shot a moose and he is letting the class take the hide. We're doing the tanning at our place. Remember?"

"Oh, yeah."

"Elders Mabel and Sam are here to teach the class about tanning hide."

"Listen up," Mabel called to the class, as Raymond slowly walked up and peered in from a safe distance. This was not his idea of a good time. He would much rather watch someone take apart a transmission, than skin an animal that had just been killed by a bullet, and had its guts ripped out.

"This is a young bull moose (yâpew)," Mabel advised. "It is in prime condition. It hasn't been doing a lot of chasing through the bush or fighting the older bulls. Okay, grab the legs and roll it onto its back. Come on. Grab a leg."

"Do we have to?"

"Yes."

"Raymond," someone yelled, "you've got big strong muscles. Grab a leg and pull."

"Okay," Raymond said, as he slowly walked up to the dead animal that was sprawled on the ground. Blood was still oozing out of its neck and its eyes were glazed over. A whiff of dead meat reached his nostrils as he and the others pulled the carcass over onto its back. He figured he was more of a gatherer than a hunter.

"This animal has been split open properly," Sam said as he pointed to the cut on the belly of the animal. "A proper cut starts between the rear legs and goes all the way up into the neck. The skin should also be cut part way up each of the legs and the tail. There isn't much of a tail, but those bones will be cut out and the hooves cut off. We'll start on the belly first, carefully pulling the skin away from the meat. Sometimes the membranes separate easily. Other times, you have to use a knife to cut the fat and the meat away from the skin. Be sure not to cut into the skin. See how it separates?" he asked, as he expertly started to skin the animal.

"Okay," Mabel said. "Who's next?"

"Raymond," Arlene called, "look after Sylvia for a bit while I try the skinning."

"Sure," Raymond said, drawing a breath of fresh air. He was sure Arlene was going to get him to do the skinning. He was glad for the excuse to play with Sylvia. She was more than a year old now and she was interested in touching and tasting everything. It would be good to keep her away from the moose carcass.

Raymond and Sylvia were laughing and chasing butterflies, when Arlene called.

"Raymond. It's your turn."

"You're not done yet?"

"No, everyone gets a turn."

"Okay," he said, as he reluctantly turned Sylvia over to her mother.

Raymond didn't realize what hard work this was.

"Women's work," he chuckled to himself.

He was careful not to cut the skin. He tried to do a good job, just like the others. When everyone had a turn to practice, and the skinning was done, Sam said, "Okay, that's it for tonight. Mabel and I will finish cutting off the tail and hooves. We'll keep the hide moist in a tub of water until tomorrow."

The skinned moose was loaded onto a truck. It would be hung in a garage for awhile to cure before being cut up and packaged for the freezer.

"Ekosi. See you tomorrow."

"Raymond," Sam called, "will you give me a hand in cutting the brain out of this moose head?"

"What?"

"We have to saw the top of the skull off and take the brain out for the tanning process. Usually, the animal's brain is sufficient to tan its hide. I could use your help."

"What a way to go!" Raymond said. "Somebody uses your brains to tan your hide."

"Okay, let's do it."

Raymond was never into that biology stuff where they dissected animals and they looked at the brains. He stuck to engines, but now he had a chance to see a brain.

"It might even be interesting to see what a brain looks like. It is probably much like ours."

"That's right. Now hold the head down while I saw through the top of the skull."

"He has a pretty thick skull. Just like some people I know," Raymond observed.

Raymond had to turn away when the brain juice started to leak out through the cut. The smell and sight conjured up a swirling, bubbling mixture in his stomach, much like a witch's brew, ready to erupt at any moment.

"I think I'm going to puke. Enohte pwâkamoyân." Raymond mumbled.

"Now, I know why I work with cars and computers instead of being a brain surgeon."

"Look at this beauty. I did a pretty good job, if I say so myself," Sam commented to Raymond who was now turning white and green around the edges.

"We'll boil it in this bucket and use it for tanning the hide tomorrow," Sam said.

"I hope it isn't one of Kohkom's soup buckets."

"No, this is my soup bucket," Sam said, with a smile.

"I've gained enough brain power for one day," Raymond said.

"Ekosi."

• • •

CHAPTER 7

"Over here!" Mabel called from behind one of the trees at Marg's place. "Help me get the moose hide out of this washtub." Raymond and Sam went to help.

"Hey," Raymond teased. "We were getting the smoking fire started. That's the men's job, right? We don't do women's work."

"Yeah," Sam agreed.

"Get your butts over here. Put those big muscles to work for a change. Pansy mechanics nowadays. All you do is replace a few computer chips and sit around drinking coffee."

"Okay, okay, you've got us figured out. We only charge for the coffee, but it's very expensive."

"You got that right; now, lift this hide out of the tub."

Gobs of moose fat and strings of sinew, clinging to bunches of long hair, swirled in the water as they grabbed onto the hide.

"I think I'm going to lose my breakfast," Raymond joked, as they rinsed the hide in fresh water. Actually, he wasn't sure it was just a joke.

"Okay, all together now. Pull this thing out of the tub," Sam instructed.

The hide was pulled out and laid hair down onto the dry, brown grass, exposing the flesh side. Most of the blood had soaked out, but the tissue that had been missed while skinning, glistened white in the early sunshine of the cool October morning. Some of the hair was starting to loosen.

"Come here," Sam called.

"Here, help me lash this pole between these two trees. Grab those other poles and we'll make a frame to tie the hide onto and then make a lean-to with it," Sam said to Raymond. "We'll put one end of the tanning frame on this cross pole and the other end on the ground."

"It seems to be pretty solid," Raymond said as he leaned on the cross pole.

Calling from the hide, Mabel got the students to gather around. She proceeded to instruct them on how to make holes parallel to the outside edge of the hide.

"Make the holes about four fingers apart and far enough in from the edge so the rope (pêminahkwân) doesn't rip out"

"Okay, everybody. Grab some of these ropes and thread them through the slits along the edge of the hide," Sam directed.

"Yes, that's right," Mabel encouraged. "Now, tie them together. Don't worry, Raymond, that's just a bit of dried moose guts (takisiya)."

"Yeah, right."

"Help me lift the hide," Sam said as he motioned to the students.

"Arlene, when we get it to the top pole, wind some of the ropes around the pole and then pull them tight," Mabel instructed. "Once we get the hide hung from the top, then we can continue tying it to the side poles and the one on the bottom."

"Don't forget the pole going across the hide about one third of the way up," Sam reminded. "This is used to stand on and to take some of a person's weight off the hide."

"You mean we're going to stand on the hide?" someone asked.

"That's right."

"Yuk."

Marg came by with a bucket of soup and she put it on the fire. She also came over to inspect the work and to help look after Sylvia. She nodded her approval.

"Okay, tighten the ropes and tie them. We want them good and tight because they will stretch," Sam said.

"Now, the women's work starts," Mabel chuckled. "Up to this point we've just been warming up."

"Huh!"

"Here is a traditional moose bone flesher, "mekihkwan,'" Mabel said as she held up a modified front leg bone of a moose. "We tie a leather strap around the top of the bone and the other end of the strap is looped around our arm like this. This way you can put your shoulder into the motion and use the weight of your body to help in the fleshing. First, we use a knife to start separating the tissue from the hide. Then we use the bone."

"It works like this," Sam said as he used the bone to make a downward stroke on the hanging hide. "We hit directly at the hide and then pull down. Work it over and over until all of the tissue is scraped off. Okay, get working."

"How do we work the top," someone asked.

"Well, the traditional women just hoisted their skirts and climbed onto the stretched hide," Mabel told them.

"Yuk!"

"That's right, Raymond," Mabel encouraged. "You have the correct motion and see how it's cleaning the hide? You do good women's work."

Raymond caught the twinkle in her eye.

Everyone had a chance to work on the hide and to practice the fleshing technique.

"Ouch! I'm getting blisters."

"This is hard work!" another complained.

"Just women's work," Arlene said, as she walked up to the group with Sylvia.

"Let Sylvia at it," Raymond offered. "She's got lots of energy."

"Yeah," Sam said. "Break her in young on this women's work."

"Lunch!" Mabel called. What a welcome sound.

"Wash up and get some bannock on your stick to bake over the fire. Marg has some delicious soup, if you're interested."

"I don't dare ask what kind it is," Raymond laughed.

The break was great, but the day was going fast and they still had lots of work to do.

“Ki nanâskomitin. Thank you for the lunch,” Mabel offered. “You didn’t need to do that.”

“I just need to practice being a good kohkom,” Marg said with a chuckle.

“Alright,” Sam said. “Stretch your muscles because we need them in good shape to turn the hide.”

"If we left the hair on, we could go to the tanning stage now, but we are going to scrape it off," Mabel informed them.

The frame was turned over and a section of the hair was removed from the neck of the hide which was on the top.

"This is a hide scraper or mataigen," Sam told the students. "It is another moose leg bone that has been fitted with a sharp scraper. We have to take off the hair and the first layer of skin. It is called scarf. Use the bone as a scraper, not a knife. We may have to sharpen it after awhile because the hair is coarse and it will make the blade dull."

"I hate this moose hair!" Raymond yelled in disgust. "It sticks to everything."

"Be careful with it," Arlene said. "I want to use it for my moose hair tufting project."

"This hair will be great for tufting," Mabel agreed.

"I'll store it in one of Raymond's boots," Arlene teased.

"Sylvia! Get that out of your mouth," Raymond scolded gently.

"She's just starting on the tufting project," Sam said slyly.

Finally, Mabel was satisfied with the hide. It was getting dry and crinkly. "This is pretty good rawhide (aâhpin), coming from beginners," she said. "Actually, the men did pretty good women's work."

"Yeah!"

"One last job today," Sam told the students. "This is an easy job, but rather messy."

"Raymond likes to mess around," Arlene laughed. "He should be good at this job."

"I'm sure he'll do a great job of rubbing in the moose brains," Mabel offered.

"Yuk!" Raymond snorted. "I have enough brains!"

"Listen up," Mabel prompted. "The term "tanning" refers to the soaking of the animal hide with the preservative "tannic acid" which keeps the skin from rotting. The historic method was "brain tanning". There is tannic acid, as well as oil and conditioners in the brain that will make the hide useful as material for making clothing, bags and moccasins."

"Okay, take your knives. We are going to cut this hide off the frame," Mabel told them. "Leave the part along the edge that has the holes and still has hair and skin."

"This is the brain that we took out of the moose," Sam said. "I boiled it with fat to make a greasy paste."

"We're just about done for today," Mabel encouraged.

"Oh," Raymond teased in jest, "it seems as if we just got started."

With the hide on the grass, hair side up, the students started rubbing and working the brain paste into every part of the hide.

"Now, we need to fold it on itself and make a package," Sam instructed. "Grab a side, Raymond, and fold it over."

The hide slid around and the brain paste oozed out around the edges. It was going on supper time, but Raymond had lost his appetite.

"Sylvia! No! Yucky!" Arlene said as she ran to grab Sylvia who tried to sample the brain paste.

"I think this is more of a de-braining session than a tanning lesson," Raymond laughed.

"Okay," Mabel said. This does it for today. We'll let the brain paste work over night and then we'll finish the job tomorrow."

"Wow," Arlene said. "One day a dummy hide and the next, an intellectual blanket."

"A real Jekyll and Hyde story," Raymond offered.

"I want all you men here early tomorrow morning." Sam announced. "We have men's work to do, to get the smoking fire ready."

"Ekosi," Mabel said as she waved goodbye to the students.

"Come and get it, penâtamok" Marg called. Fresh moose meat and bannock is ready."

"Thanks, Marg," Mabel said. "Most of these students have to go home now, but Sam and I will be glad to stop in for some moose and bannock. She wasn't sure how many of the students would want to taste moose meat after today.

"Raymond!" Arlene called. "Bring Sylvia. We're going to Marg's for moose meat and bannock."

"Okay," Raymond said.

"Come, Sylvia. We're going to Kohkom's."

"Com Com," Sylvia stuttered.

Raymond always enjoyed going to Marg's for moose meat and bannock, but this time he was sure he could smell fish guts.

Marg and the elders started talking about the old ways. Sometimes they switched to Cree. Raymond could only understand part of it, but he learned things about Kohkom and Mosôm that he had never heard before. They had had a hard life, hunting, trapping, skinning and tanning hide. Mosôm also had to work hauling freight and fighting forest fires, to keep his family from starving. Sylvia snuggled into Marg's arms and fell asleep.

"Thank you for telling me more about my family. I'm proud of all of you!" Raymond said as he picked up Sylvia from Marg's arms. "It's time I get the girls home," he said, as he winked at Arlene.

"You go ahead," Arlene said with a teasing smile, "I'm having too much fun here."

"Good night, wâpahki kawâpamitinâwâw," they all said as everyone got ready to leave.

• • •

CHAPTER 8

The fire felt good on this cool morning. Raymond and the other men were happy to warm themselves by the fire.

"Tânisi," Sam greeted the scruffy looking bunch of male students. "Okay, this is men's work. Get the saws moving and the axes swinging. We're going to need some wood and a lot of spruce boughs."

"I thought we wanted smoke, not fire?" Raymond questioned.

"You'll see. Come with me."

Sam took the men on a trek through the willows, stopping at a clump with many dead branches, their trunks covered with moss.

"Chop up some of these rotten, punky stumps and take them back to the fire," Sam instructed. "If you see any mushroom-like things, wihkwaskwa (bracket fungi) hanging on the trunks of the diamond willows, save them. They are used in smudging ceremonies."

"Raymond, come with me."

Sam and Raymond went into a stand of black spruce and they trimmed a few of the lower branches. They also dug up some chunks of rotten punky black spruce.

"That should do it," Sam said when they had two large piles.

"Over here, guys!" Raymond called. "Help us pack this stuff up to the fire."

When they had finished carrying supplies, they gathered around the fire. Sam started explaining what they were going to do.

"It takes different types of fire for the different stages of the tanning process. Sometimes, it takes a flaming fire and sometimes, we just want the heat and smoke of a small fire."

"Hi, guys!" Arlene called. "Raymond, look after Sylvia while I help Mabel unload her stuff. Keep her away from the fire. She'll probably want to touch and taste it."

"Arlene!" Sam called. "We'll need some warm, soapy water as well. Can you get some for us, please?"

"Okay."

"Over here, guys!" Mabel called.

"We were just enjoying the fire. Now, I suppose we have do women's work again," Raymond said with a smile.

"That's right, but I don't know if you can keep up to these women for two days in a row," Mabel chuckled. "Help me with this hide."

"Now, guys," Sam said, "we need to take the hide out of the tub and open it up."

"What's that terrible smell?" Raymond choked as Sam opened up the hide and the moose brain paste slithered from between the layers. "I'm going to be sick."

"That is just the smell of brains doing their job with the tannic acid."

"Okay, guys," Mabel said, "lay some of those spruce boughs flat over the fire to make a smoke."

"Cough! Cough!"

"I never was much of a smoker," Raymond sputtered.

"Now, help me spread the hide over the boughs to give it the first smoke treatment. This helps the brains and grease soak in. Rub it to make sure it doesn't get too hot. Lift it up if it does. We don't want any burns."

"Here's the water," Arlene puffed as she set the heavy bucket down.

"Raymond, pour the water into the tub," Sam directed.

"We'll take turns washing the hide in the soapy water. Now that the brains have done their job, we need to get it all out and replaced with water. You'll have to work it back and forth to get the greasy brain paste out of the pores of the hide. It will take a lot of washing."

Raymond took his turn, but it was just about the last straw for this tanning business. How did he get hooked up in this anyway? Oh, yes, Arlene.

"We did all that work putting the brains in and now we're going to take them out?"

"That's right."

"That looks like it will do it," Mabel offered.

"Now, we need to run the hide through this metal hoop with the flesh side out. This will help loosen any remaining tissue and make the hide softer."

Back and forth the hide went. Everybody took a turn. Eventually, the grease and brains were replaced by water.

"Hang it over the pole between these two trees," Mabel said.

"Get the scrapers," Sam told the students, "and gently scrape the water off the hide."

"My arms don't move anymore," someone complained.

"How much more slime do we have?" Raymond asked, tongue in cheek.

"Just enough for your lunch," someone said sarcastically.

"The hide looks good," Sam observed.

"Okay," Mabel instructed, "fold the hide over like this, starting on both sides and work toward the middle."

The result was a long, flimsy tube of wet hide.

Sam and Mabel showed the group how to wrap it around a tree and to loop it onto itself. A pole was inserted into the loop and the pole was turned to tighten the loop.

"Help!" Mabel called. "Bring your muscles over here. We need help turning this pole. It squeezes the water out of the hide."

"This hide is going to be worn out before it ever gets to be used for moccasins," Raymond speculated.

After the wringing, the hide had to be pulled apart and stretched into shape. It was swung back and forth over a flaming fire to warm and to dry but not to burn.

Surprisingly, the hide was now soft and pliable. All that was left to do was the final smoking to finish the tanning process and to give it a rich brown colour.

"Come and get it!" Marg called as she came with strips of smoked fish and fresh bannock biscuits.

Raymond was hungry and the fish was a good change from moose.

They all gathered around the fire to eat lunch.

The hot coals were glowing with intermittent bursts of blue, red and yellow colours. The odd spark snapped and leapt from the fire pit. Raymond studied the change in the shape and outlines of the wood as it was consumed by the fire. It changed from solid fibres into gaseous wisps that soon burst into flame and then disappeared.

"Life is like that," Raymond offered.

"Like what?"

"Life is like wood in a fire. It starts out as a strong, solid framework that can be used to carry out many useful activities, but, over time, as it is heated in the course of living, the strong fibres are changed to a less useful form and eventually they will become a vapour that vanishes like a wisp of smoke, lost forever in the currents of the atmosphere."

"Why do you say that?" Sam inquired.

"Well, look at Kohkom," Raymond said, while pointing to Kohkom who was returning to her cabin with the empty bucket. "She was a strong woman, working hard on the trap line, and now, she mostly stands by and watches. Her dreams are like this smoke, swirling away into the atmosphere."

"A long time ago, an Elder and wise man named Solomon felt the same way, but, in the end, he saw hope in the cycles of life."

"I wonder if Mosôm saw hope in the cycles of life," Raymond mused.

"Hello there, handsome," Rose called to Raymond, as she walked up to the fire.

"Where did you come from?" Raymond asked in a surprised voice.

"From Kohkom," Rose replied slyly.

"Okay, okay."

"Allen and I came out to help Marg get the fish ready. Allen is inspecting the hide. We want to know how to do this if we go to live in the bush someday."

"Yeah, right," Raymond laughed. "Thanks for helping Kohkom."

"Com Com," Sylvia called as she ran to Rose.

"Hi, Sweety," Rose said as she swooped Sylvia up in her arms."

"She thinks she's special, having a câ pân and more kohkoms," Arlene laughed.

"She is special and so are all of you," Raymond noted.

"Hey, muscles!" Mabel called. "We need to get this hide ready for smoking. We need to sew the hide into a sack by stitching the sides together and closing in the top. The bottom will be left open and the sack will be suspended over the smoking fire. A cloth will be sewn on the bottom to protect the hide from the ground and the fire."

Everyone helped get the hide ready for the final smoking.

"Okay, guys, now is the time to put the punky black spruce on the fire," Sam told them. "The fire is just right. No flames, but a nice bed of coals."

The chunks were added to the fire and the thick coils of blue and black smoke danced from side to side and blanketed everyone in a haze of smoke.

"The smoke is everywhere," Arlene complained.

"You're like a smoke magnet," Raymond teased. "Wherever you go the smoke follows. Stay away from Arlene!"

"It likes you, too. See, now it's going your way."

"Everybody, grab onto the hide sack," Sam instructed. "We'll carry it over to the fire and hang it from the pole above."

Smoke billowed out from under the hide and caught everyone in the face, making it difficult to breathe.

"Cough!"

"Choke!"

"Yucky," Sylvia sputtered.

"We're all going to have smoked hide, just like the moose," Raymond joked.

"I like the smell," Arlene offered. "It smells like the moccasins Kohkom gave us."

"You're right, as usual."

Even though everyone was dirty and tired, they were having a fun social time, just as in the olden days.

"The day is getting late," Mabel told the group. "If you have to go, it is okay. Some of us will stay around for the evening. We have to turn the hide inside out to smoke both sides. Later, we will take it down from the pole and check to see if it has a good colour. If it needs more smoking, we can swing it back and forth into the smoke until it is tanned and coloured the way we want it. You've done a super job. I think the hide will be beautiful."

"Ka wâpamitin âsamîna, good bye," Sam called to those leaving. "You've been a hard-working bunch.

Sometime soon we'll cut the hide and you'll all get a piece to keep. Oh, by the way, no class tomorrow."

"Ki nanâskomitinân, thank you," they called back.

"So what do you think?" Raymond asked Kohkom, who was standing a short distance away, watching the proceedings.

"Sam and Mabel are doing a good job. This is how I used to do it, but now this old woman can only watch. Mosôm and I had to work hard."

"See you tomorrow," Raymond said as he watched her shuffle off to her cabin, sorry that she now had to face aging alone.

"What really happened to Mosôm, anyway?" Raymond wondered.

Raymond's muscles ached and his body smelled of smoky sweat and half-rotten moose brains, but he was glad for the chance to learn some of the old ways. He was also glad that Arlene had enjoyed the day. Maybe they could do this on their own sometime. Arlene could make moccasins and sew things for Sylvia. He was glad, too, that Sylvia had a chance to touch the hide, to feel the moose brains and to become bathed in the smoke from the tanning fire. She was the latest part in his cycle of life. Even Kohkom had a good day, watching a process she had done many times and also feeling useful by cooking the fish and bannock.

"Wow!" Raymond commented to Arlene as they walked home. "I have a lot more appreciation for the work Kohkom and Mosôm did in their day." He made no mention of his impending session in the city.

The howling of the dogs reminded Raymond that he had been neglecting them for a few days. The howl of Shadow brought back memories of the time he had crashed his snowmobile on Dog Island.

"Down Shadow! Down!"

• • •

CHAPTER 9

Raymond in the city

Raymond liked his small town in northern Alberta. He knew a lot of people. Actually, he was related to a lot of them. As a mechanic, he knew people who came to the shop. He actually remembered them by the make and model of the vehicle they drove and he could tell anyone what he had fixed on their car or truck. He also knew people from the college that Arlene worked with and had gone to school with. Of course, some had been his classmates at school.

Most of the people Raymond knew were friendly and happy. Sure, there were those who were pushy, rude and prejudiced, both white toward Aboriginal and Aboriginal toward white, but most were trying to look after their families and to be good citizens of the community. Yes, some were dealing with addictions and homelessness, but there were people and agencies in town that were helping those in need.

On the occasions that Raymond had to go to the city for his apprenticeship class, the only person he knew was Jack and some others who had stayed in the same house. He befriended some of his classmates, but many were aloof and very competitive. He sensed a bit of jealousy when he, an Aboriginal, got the highest marks. Most times, Raymond felt lost and overwhelmed by the throngs of people on the streets and in the shopping malls. He learned to travel around the city by vehicle and bus, but he preferred just to walk. Raymond was appalled by the number of Aboriginal people who were homeless and walking the streets. They seemed to have lost their way in the world. He wondered if the negative impact of the Residential School system, that many of the Elders endured, would eventually dwindle. They had no connection to their Aboriginal culture, but they didn't fit into the white man's world. Some Aboriginals faced prejudice when they tried to find work and accommodation. He was glad he could stay with Jack. Maybe this was why Rose gave up the old ways and she wasn't happy about his wanting to learn more about his culture. The more injustice he saw, the more distain he felt for the white man's ways.

"Raymond!" Arlene yelled as she ran to him, threw her arms around him and kissed him. Sylvia came toddling along behind. Raymond scooped her into his arms and he hugged both of his women.

"What are you doing here?"

"We knew you were finishing your course today, and we wanted to celebrate with you. We hear you got top marks," Allen said.

"How would you like to go to a posh restaurant in the west end?" Rose asked.

"Mom and Dad offered to bring Sylvia and me into the city to see you," Arlene explained. "How do you like your surprise?"

"Great!"

"Okay, everybody. Hop in and we'll go for dinner," Allen instructed.

• • •

"Wow, this is posh," Raymond whispered as they entered the fancy west end hotel dining room.

"Yeah, this is no cheap café like we're used to," Arlene whispered back.

"I'm glad Mom and Dad are paying the bill."

"Yeah, we'll have to mind our manners."

"Oh, no! Sylvia!"

Sylvia, with her Aboriginal complexion, and her black hair tied into in a wiggly top knot on top of her head, was running and dancing among the tables and the other guests. Raymond finally captured her and he got a child seat from a waitress. However, Sylvia, a little girl used to her freedom at Kohkom's, objected vigorously to being strapped into a children's chair. The adults finalized their order and then they tried to entertain Sylvia. Some of the other diners even helped provide the entertainment, but Raymond noticed that one couple seemed to be looking irate. He took Sylvia out of the chair to give her a break, but he lost her as soon as her little feet hit the floor. She was gone, straight to the irate couple, under one side of their table and out the other. Raymond was in hot pursuit, weaving in and around other tables before he grabbed her and headed back to his table. As they passed the irate couple, the lady spoke up.

"Why don't you take the little Indian back to the reserve where she belongs?"

Surprisingly, it was Rose who answered.

"The little Indian is on the reserve," Rose said in a quivering voice as she pointed to the sign. It read, First Nation Hotel.

"Let's get out of here!" the lady retorted, as she grabbed the man's arm and they marched out the door.

Raymond had to grab Arlene, as well as to hold onto Sylvia. Arlene was so mad, Raymond could envision smoke coming out of her ears.

"It's okay," Raymond said, trying to calm her down. "Some people are like that. That's their problem."

"Well, that woman will have another problem if I see her again."

"Let it go!"

It was easier to let it go, once the waiter brought the food and drink. Everyone settled down and they enjoyed the meal, even Sylvia. The evening of food and fun with family left Raymond happy to have such a great family. However, the incident with the white woman left an after taste that added to his distain for the white man's ways.

Raymond was glad to return home with his family and to leave the confusion of the city. It was easy returning to his life as a mechanic and family man, but questions about Mosôm still lingered. The call of the island still haunted him, inviting him to come and to live by the old ways. Lately he heard a voice calling, "North of Dog Island."

• • •

CHAPTER 10

"I see Marg got a big load of firewood," Raymond teased as he greeted Arlene and Sylvia.

"That's not firewood," Arlene retorted. "Don't you remember? The college is holding the log cabin building course here behind Kohkom's place."

"The logs look like they've already been burned."

"They have. Well, not completely burned. These logs were salvaged from the Grizzly fire. They were fire killed by the heat and most of the bark was burned off."

"Why are there light and dark spots on some of them?"

"We were told that the extreme heat created a spotted layer called leopard skin."

"I still think they would make nice, dry firewood."

"Well, it is best to use dry logs to build with. That way, most of the shrinking has already happened before you make the cuts and notches."

"I see Mabel and Sam are here now."

"Hi, guys," Sam said as he dropped a load of saws and axes.

"Here are the plans and dimensions," Mabel informed.

"Why do you need plans for cutting firewood?" Raymond teased and winked at Arlene.

"Arlene," Mabel spoke up, "can you keep this mechanic away from the logs?"

"No. We need his big muscles. Just give him a wrench and keep him away from the saws."

Everyone laughed. Actually, Raymond was happy to help and to learn how to build a log cabin like the one Mosôm had built for Kohkom.

"Those hand saws and axes look like a lot of work. I know where I can get a good chain saw," Raymond teased.

"We're learning the old ways. Remember?" Sam reminded him.

"Hi, guys," the class of young adults called as they spilled out of the College van. They were ready to go to work. They had had enough of the classroom and they were ready for the hands on experience.

"Sylvia!" Arlene called. "Get away from those logs. Yucky! We'll watch from over here."

"I'll watch her," Kohkom offered as she walked up from the cabin. "You and Raymond can join the class."

"Thanks," Raymond said. "I'd like to learn how to build my own log house, like Mosôm did."

"You work hard like Mosôm, and you'll learn. Come, Sylvia. We'll look for some tea."

"Listen up," Mabel called, "we're going to give you guys an overview of log cabin building. Some things will be like the old ways, but for some things we'll use modern equipment."

"That's right," Sam told the group. "If we use some of the modern tools, we'll explain what they used in the old days."

"Follow me," Mabel directed. "This is where we'll be working for a few days," she said, pointing to a small clearing in the tall grass. "The most important part of any building is its foundation. We have placed some concrete blocks at the corners to keep the logs off the ground. We'll place the sill logs on these corner blocks and then add the others, alternating the end logs with the side logs."

Sam explained the various tools, procedures and safety measures including the use of hard hats and steel toed boots.

"Okay, find two nice straight logs from the pile and we'll use the lug hooks with people using the handles on each side of a log. Carry the logs over here and lay one on each side next to the blocks."

Both the young men and women helped carry the logs.

"Oh, that hurts!" someone said as he skinned his shin.

"Ouch!" another said as a sliver went under her finger nail.

They all agreed this was hard work, but they wanted to learn about the old ways.

"The downside of the sill log needs to be flat," Sam informed the group. "We do this by chopping off or hewing, as it is called, one side of the log with the broad axe. This one has a large blade and an offset handle to protect the knuckles. We sometimes use this axe called an adz," Sam said as he picked up a different axe. "The blade of this one is horizontal and you swing it between your legs."

"That could be hard on your toes, shins and other things," Raymond offered.

"You are absolutely right."

Large tongs were also used to drag logs and a peavey was used to turn them over. Log dogs kept the logs from rolling over and a drawknife helped peel off bark that was still on the logs. Bucksaws and chisels helped make cuts and notches and a hand auger made holes if the logs needed to be pegged together.

"Raymond," Sam called. "Get your group to carry one of those shorter logs over here. The short ones are for the ends of the cabin."

"Okay, Raymond," someone said, "put those mechanic muscles to work."

"I can't find a wrench."

With the log dogs holding the end log, which was sitting on top of the side logs, Mabel demonstrated how to fit the logs together.

"This is like a big compass from your geometry set," Mabel explained.

"Oh, no!" Raymond exclaimed. "Not geometry!" Actually, Raymond was glad to be able to put his math skills to work in the real world, whether as a mechanic or as a carpenter.

"This big compass with a level on it is called a scribe," Mabel continued. "We use it to mark the size and shape of the notch needed to fit one log onto the other. There are many different ways to notch logs and different ways to finish the ends. We'll demonstrate the most common ones."

"We'll use this small level, attached to a line, to make sure the building is level," Sam said. "In the old days, they just put some oil in a small bottle of water. The oil would float and a line was marked on the bottle to show level. A string, with the bottle attached, was then strung along the top log and the log notched in a way that made it level."

The marked log was removed and Sam demonstrated how to notch it and to fit the two logs together. He demonstrated other types of notches that were used on the ends of the logs, such as the saddle notch, tenon-joint notch and the dovetail notch.

"Logs are scribed, cut and notched differently, depending on how you want to chink the space between the logs," Mabel explained. "The modern way is to cut in grooves and to place a tube of insulation into the groove before putting on the next log. In the old days, they used mud and moss or manure mixed with mortar."

"Okay," Sam encouraged, "everybody gets a chance to try doing a notch."

Over the next few classes, more logs were added by using a simple ramp and pulley to roll the new log on top of the previous logs. Floor joists for the floor boards were added and openings made for a door and a window. The logs were aligned and spiked with long spikes to keep them in place. The top side logs were shaped as plate logs, allowing the roof rafter logs to fit in.

• • •

"Listen up, guys," Mabel called. "It's time for another math lesson. We're ready to put on the roof and we have to figure out the slope. Every roof has the shape of a triangle. We just need to decide what the rise and run will be. A common slope is a four inch rise for every twelve inches of run. You can find this by using a carpenter's square. We'll mark and cut the ends of each of the small roof logs to have this angle and then cut a notch in the other end to fit over the plate log."

Gable ends were framed with logs and rough lumber. A long log was fitted into the gable ends to form the peak of the roof. The log rafters were cut, notched and raised using a block and tackle hoist. This formed the frame of the roof. Everything was spiked into place.

"In the old days," Mabel told the students, "the roof was made of close fitting logs and covered with moss and sod. Sometimes, layers of roll roofing were placed on top and held down with small logs. We'll use OSB (Oriented Strand Board) for the decking and asphalt shingles."

"This is really looking good," Sam commended the students for their work. "You've done a fine job. We've made a simple, small building, but now that you know the basics, you could build your own, fancy house."

• • •

"Thanks for the bannock," Raymond told Kohkom.

"Yes," Arlene said, while watching Sylvia devour her piece of bannock.

Kohkom looked tired from entertaining Sylvia. The years on the trap line had taken their toll and the wrinkled face and gnarled fingers were showing the effects. Her vest exhibited scenes of Aboriginal culture and her moccasins displayed her colourful and exceptionally skillful bead work. Kohkom could still bake bannock for all to enjoy and entertain people with her stories and legends from the past. Sylvia, with her fresh face, black hair, and sparkling eyes, was a portrait of a younger Marg.

Raymond and Arlene enjoyed listening to the stories about Kokhom and Mosôm and their life on the trap line, living by the old ways. They were becoming more and more dissatisfied with the fast pace and consumer driven ways of town and city living.

"We wish we could live on the land by the old ways, as you and Mosôm did," Raymond told Marg.

"Would it be possible for us to try doing that for a year or so?" Arlene asked.

"I'm not sure that is possible any more," Kohkom said. "It is a lot of hard work and many trap lines are crossed by cut lines and truck traffic."

"What about Mosôm's trap line on Dog Island?" Raymond asked.

"His trap line on the island is now part of the Park. He also had some trap lines on the North Shore, but those are all gone."

"Fur coats and jackets are very expensive, so we should make lots of money," Arlene surmised.

"That's true, but for all of the hard work, we never made much money," Marg told them. "Mosôm always made sure we had enough moose meat and fish to eat. We could buy flour, so we could always cook moose meat and bannock. In the spring and summer, Mosôm worked for forestry, fighting fires."

"You don't know much about hunting and trapping," Arlene reminded Raymond.

"I learned some things from my dad, you know."

"I know what you can do," Kohkom remembered, her wrinkles smoothing into a pleasant smile.

"What?" Raymond asked with anticipation.

"We have a relative living on a trap line north of Sandy Lake. We call him Uncle Henry. He might like to have a big, strong man helping out for a while. I'm sure he'd be glad to show you how to hunt and to trap."

"That would be great."

"He still uses a dog team, but he also uses the modern traps and he has a snowmobile."

"You could use Shadow and the dogs," Arlene suggested. "Your snowmobile still needs a little work on it."

"You did have to remind me about that, didn't you?"

"Sylvia's sleeping. We have to go."

"We both had a big day," Marg chuckled.

"Can you contact this Uncle Henry?"

"I'll talk to one of our relatives up North."

"How do you know who to talk to?"

"They're all my relatives," Kokhom said and everyone laughed.

"Good night."

• • •

CHAPTER 11

"Grab a hunk of moose meat from the ice house," Uncle Henry called to Raymond. "There's a bag of smoked fish somewhere in there as well. We'll need two days of food for us and the dogs. If we snare a rabbit, we can have fresh stew."

"Hike!" Raymond called to the dogs, as he headed them down to the ice house.

Raymond and Uncle Henry were starting out onto the trap line after the first, big snowfall and they were planning to stay overnight at a small temporary camp along the way. Uncle Henry was using three sled dogs in line, harnessed to a dog sled, to carry the food and other supplies for the trip. The dogs each needed about a kilogram of dried fish every day. The other supplies included various lures and baits, an axe, a small saw, wire cutters, rolls of different sized brass wire for snares, a screen and trowel for covering traps, along with safety equipment and survival gear. Winter sleeping bags rounded out the load.

"Here, help me throw these bags of traps onto the snowmobile," Uncle instructed Raymond. "I'll take the dogs ahead and you can bring the machine. I already packed the trails last week, but this snow is pretty deep. In the old days, we had to snowshoe ahead of the dogs to break trail. Now, if the dogs tire out, we can go ahead with the snowmobile and pack the snow."

"Great! I thought you were going to make me run along behind," Raymond laughed.

"We still use a lot of the old ways for trapping, but some things are more modern. Most trappers now use a snowmobile for some of their trap lines. We no longer use the old style foot-hold traps. Now, we use killing traps and snares to prevent suffering for the trapped animals. Traps, like the conibear type, use strong springs to squeeze the animal, causing them to pass out and then to die."

"That's good," Raymond said. "I don't like to see animals suffer. I don't like blood and guts much either."

"You'll get used to it by the time you're done here."

Raymond wasn't so sure. Kohkom had arranged for Raymond to come to Uncle Henry's trap line north of Sandy Lake. Raymond took some time off work at the garage and he was now headed out onto the trap line.

"Do you have the rifles?" Uncle called.

"Yep."

"Ammo?"

"Yep. Hey, I like the chain saw strapped on the back of this snowmobile. That's my kind of wood chopping," Raymond joked.

"Mine too. Chalk one up for white man."

"Hike!" Uncle called. The dogs strained in the harness and the sled sprang to life with snow flying up and over the driver. Uncle Henry was a big man, rugged in the face with a deep set jaw, which easily melted into a friendly smile. With a strong upper body, he worked the handles on the sled and he guided the dogs along the trail, the sides of his beaver fur hat flapping in the wind. Once in awhile, he would step off and run to give the dogs a break, but he soon got back on with laboured breathing and a bit of wheezing. His lungs and legs had suffered from the harsh conditions of the trap line and the bush. Age was also taking its toll.

Raymond fired up Uncle's snowmobile and followed the dogs. This was a much newer machine than the one Raymond had. It had lots of power to carry Raymond, the traps and spare equipment. The main cabin, standing along the shore of the white, frozen lake soon faded from view. Raymond was a big man like Uncle, but his lungs and body were still young and filled with the exuberance of youth. His teenage complexion had long disappeared and his face expressed strength and confidence, his large muscles completely in control of the surging machine. The hood of his snowmobile suit was tucked tightly under his helmet. The visor sheltered his face from the wind chill and protected his eyes from the glare of the sun off the snow. A blizzard of snow billowed out behind the snowmobile as it spun in the soft snow and powered its way along the trail.

"Whoa!" Uncle called to the dogs.

Raymond pulled up beside the dogs and he viewed the large lake created by a beaver dam. He could hear the trickling of the overflow by the dam and he saw a stand of young aspen trees with branches that had been chewed and dropped into the water. Other trees had the telltale signs of beaver teeth around the trunk. Some branches had been partly skinned by a beaver as it had scraped off the living layer under the bark to provide the food necessary to survive the cold winter. Some of the branches were frozen beneath the ice and they were available to the beaver family from the water, under the ice, providing both food and protection. A huge lodge of sticks and mud rose out of the lake. This snow covered mound was a haven for the beaver family. It provided a shelter from the freezing wind chill of the winter storms, warm air for breathing and sleeping and a tunnel into the water when it was necessary to get food.

"This is a good place to set a trap for amisk," Uncle told Raymond.

"Why?"

"Well, see the steam coming out of the hole in the lodge?"

"Yes."

"That tells me this is an active colony."

"How big is it?"

"I'd say it is a fairly large colony and by the looks of all the feeding going on, they are going to run out of food before the winter is over. If we trap one or two, the rest will have a better chance of surviving. As long as we trap from the surplus, then we can keep trapping here every year. If we get greedy and take too many animals, the colony will be gone."

"Is that what happened in the past?"

"Yes. Trapping was very important to all Canadians in the early days, but greed pushed some trappers to take too many animals and then they were gone. The beaver is making a good recovery in Alberta."

"Will this be a good year for selling furs?"

"I don't know. It depends on the market and the fashion industry. Sometimes, fur is in demand; sometimes not. Some people don't want us to kill animals for their fur. For some of us, it's our way of life."

"Well, I don't like killing things, but I see that the fur trade is still very important to our people."

"You take the machine up along the trail. There's a tree across the trail up ahead. You can cut it up and then come back," Uncle instructed Raymond. "I'll give the dogs a rest and start setting up a beaver trap."

Raymond traveled along the trail, admiring the spruce trees with their branches laden down with clumps of fresh snow. Some spilled down onto his head as he passed under. Sunlight sparkled from the reflective surface of the hoar frost hanging on the fine branches of the birch trees. Raymond found the tree and he turned off the snowmobile. He stopped to listen for the silence of the forest. It was broken only by the distant drilling of a woodpecker or the crack of a tree splitting from the expanding ice in its trunk. Raymond relished the sounds and sights of the bush and was convinced that he should bring his family here. He wanted to let them enjoy the solitude and fresh smells of the forest. He wanted to get away from the town and city life with its continuous noise, stress and prejudice. "This is how Mosôm lived," Raymond thought. The silence was shattered when he started using the chainsaw to cut the fallen tree into sections and to throw the pieces off the trail. When he finished, he returned to the beaver pond.

"Over here!" Uncle called and he motioned for Raymond to join him on the ice.

"What are you doing?"

"I'm using this ice chipper to make a hole for the trap."

The ice chipper was a length of heavy metal that had a sharp knife welded on one end and a rope attached on the other. It could slice through the hard ice and chip out a hole. If the bar accidentally slipped down the hole, a pull on the rope would bring it back.

"Look at this pile of branches. See the fresh cutting on this side?" Uncle rasped between gasps of breath.

"Yes. The beaver have been feeding here, but I don't see any trails," Raymond observed.

"Look at the ice. See the bubbles? There is a tunnel here that the animals are using to swim from the lodge to the food pile. I'm chopping a hole into it and we'll put one of these bigger conibears into the tunnel. When an animal swims through, it will be trapped. Later, when we come back, we'll chop it out of the ice."

"Here, let me chop for awhile," Raymond offered.

When the hole was large enough, Uncle started showing Raymond how to safely set the trap.

"These springs are very strong and they could break your fingers if you get them caught in the striker bars. We use the safety gripper to keep the striker bars from closing, should the trigger trip before we're ready. This little hack saw tied to my coat is there in case I need to cut the spring. We place the trap setter hooks into the eyelets of the spring and close the trap setter with the spring compressed. Then, we put the safety hook on and release the setter. Okay, you do the other side."

"I don't know about this. I'm glad you have the hack saw," Raymond said with a nervous chuckle.

Raymond had no problem working the spring with his big muscles, but it took sensitive and steady fingers to place the trap setter hook into the eyelet of the spring.

"Good work," Uncle encouraged.

Raymond realized that even though Uncle didn't have a lot of schooling, he was an excellent trapper. He would have a doctorate in trapping if there was such a thing. Raymond was anxious to learn more. He wanted to be an expert like his uncle, his father and grandfather and great grandfathers before them.

"Okay, we'll place the trap up and down in the tunnel and carefully position the trigger and adjust the dog. Only after everything is set, should you remove the safety hooks and gripper. Bring me some of those fresh cuttings and that chunk of dry alder."

"Here you go."

"This chunk of wood will hold the trap in place and the fresh cuttings will serve as bait. Over night, this will freeze into place and it will be ready for a beaver that may be in a hurry to get to the dinner table. He'll ignore the danger signs."

"Like me going after Kohkom's moose meat and bannock."

"Speaking of bannock, let's get going to the stop over cabin and have some lunch."

In the afternoon, Uncle showed Raymond how to set different types of traps, including snares for squirrels and rabbits (snowshoe hare), baited trap boxes specifically sized for mink, marten and weasels, and a natural cubby set for lynx.

"Animals are smart," Uncle said. "We have to cover our scent and leave the site as natural as possible."

He used the screen and a spruce branch to sweep snow over the set. Then they backed away from the set, covering their tracks as they went.

"It looks just like it did before," Raymond offered.

"It may look good to us, but the animals know something is different. However, one of them may be a bit careless and take our bait."

Rounding a bend in the trail, Uncle motioned for Raymond to stop.

"Look at these tracks."

"It looks like a wolf."

"You're right. Look again."

"There is more than one."

"Yep. Look again."

"Some tracks go off the trail while others stay on the trail. The animals off the trail may scare a deer or something onto the trail and the others will take it down."

"That's right. You're becoming a good bushman. There's more."

"Here is where the alpha male of the pack left his mark and scent."

"You're right. Wolves travel in families or packs and the alpha male establishes the territory. They usually have a large territory and travel around until they make a kill. Then they may stay with the kill for a few days eating and chasing off the other free loading coyotes, ravens, and gray jays or whisky jacks. If you are trapping carnivores and scavengers, this a good place to set your traps."

"Aren't wolves dangerous?"

"Wolves can be dangerous and we should be cautious, but, usually, they smell us a long time before we see them. They are naturally afraid of humans and if they have food, we don't have to worry."

"That's nice to know."

"Look again."

Raymond looked around, but he couldn't see any other signs.

"Look here," Uncle said, as he motioned for Raymond to come. "What do you see?"

"A little deer track."

"You're right. The pack may have separated the young one from its mother and it may be dinner for the wolves tonight."

"That's sad."

"That's the way of the bush."

Raymond led the way back to the dogs and snowmobile. A sudden flutter of wings startled him and then there was a loud bang.

"What happened?" Raymond asked Uncle.

"I just shot a chicken for our supper."

"But I saw it fly off."

"Oh, I shot the one that didn't fly off."

A quick pull on the wings of the ruffed grouse exposed the plump breast meat.

"Let's go," Uncle said. "We'll eat the breast and the rest will be bait for tomorrow."

Raymond was being initiated into the ways of a trapper and he had the greatest of teachers.

• • •

"So, how do you like trapping?" Uncle asked Raymond as they sipped their tea after a meal of chicken and bannock. The crackling fire spread its warmth throughout the small cabin.

"It's a whole lot different from working on engines."

"You're doing great. We have it easy tonight. Get a good rest. Tomorrow night we'll be skinning animals, I hope."

"Did you know my grandfather Alphonse?" Raymond asked timidly.

"I didn't know him, but I heard he was a great trapper and dog team racer."

"They tell me he disappeared in a blizzard on Dog Island, but I don't think that is the full story."

"That's what I heard too. I also heard that Alphonse and the medicine man on the north shore of Slave Lake didn't like each other much. Some say the man worked magic, but that was a long time ago. You get some sleep now."

"Yeah, right."

Raymond was having trouble getting to sleep thinking about Grandpa. Uncle started snoring. The floor was hard and he missed Arlene and Sylvia. He was having second thoughts about coming up here to live by the old ways. He'd have to modernize things a fair bit.

"What was that?" Raymond asked, as he jumped up. "I've never heard a howl like that."

"That's the alpha mahikan letting us know we're in his territory. Go to sleep."

"I'm trying."

Somehow, Raymond dozed off to sleep with the dogs barking and the wolf and coyotes howling in the distance.

• • •

The next day, the men were busy setting traps on the other part of the trap line and checking traps that had been set the day before. "You pack the rest of the trail," Uncle instructed. "I'm going to take the dogs and check the beaver trap. Meet me there."

"Okay," Raymond called as he throttled the machine along the trail.

When he had finished packing the trail, Raymond headed back to the beaver trap. Rounding the corner, what he saw took his breath away and punched a cramp into his stomach. Uncle was slumped over on the ice near the beaver trap. Raymond jumped off the machine and ran past the dogs. He yelled to Uncle.

"Uncle! Uncle! What happened?" Raymond asked in a breathless voice as he ran up to Uncle Henry.

"This beaver bit me," Uncle whispered with a strained smile.

"Get real! You're in trouble!"

"Yeah, my ticker isn't what it used to be. Every now and then, when I over work, I get these terrible pains in my chest. The Doc calls it angina. I have some pills in my pack, but I can't get to them. They're in a medicine bottle in the left pocket."

"I'll get them! Let go of that stupid beaver!" Raymond yelled as he went to get the pills.

"Are these nitroglycerin pills?" Raymond asked as he opened the bottle for Uncle.

"Yeah. I'll be okay in a few minutes if I keep one under my tongue for awhile. Hey, grab this stupid beaver. I don't want to lose it. It's a nice size, with good fur."

Raymond grabbed the carcass, not knowing exactly how to treat it. The big striking bars had done their job. The animal had died quickly from lack of oxygen, not drowning.

"Roll it in the snow a few times to freeze dry it and then throw it onto the snowmobile," Uncle said as he slowly got to his feet."

"Are you sure you're okay?"

"Yeah, let's get this beaver back to the main cabin. I'll take a rest and then show you how to skin and to dry a beaver pelt."

• • •

Raymond had seen Marg skin a beaver once, but he didn't like it any better this time while watching Uncle. At least this was a fresh animal and there wasn't much blood and guts.

"See how I use the knife to separate the skin from the fat. You can't turn a poor pelt into a good one, but poor handling will turn a good pelt into a bad one," Uncle instructed Raymond. "The air in the fur and all this fat keeps the animal warm in the cold water."

The yellowish fat glistened in the lantern light as Uncle made the final separation of the pelt.

"Have you ever eaten beaver tail?" Uncle asked Raymond.

"No."

"Well, it is a favourite among the old people. I'll give you a taste, but we'll save most of it to give away."

Raymond thought maybe Uncle should give it all away.

"You know how to do fleshing?"

"I've done that on a moose hide."

"That's great. You can work on the pelt and I'll look for a stretching board."

When the fleshing was finished, the pelt was stretched on a somewhat rounded board and pinned down to dry. It had beautiful dark, thick fur. Raymond admired the end product, but still had reservations about killing the animals. It would take some time before he was a trapper like Uncle.

• • •

The days went by quickly and the work was hard. They had taken a few squirrels, a lynx, a weasel with a beautiful white pelt (ermine) and two beaver. Not a lot, but the trappers were happy.

"Well, this is the last day," Uncle reminded Raymond.

"Yeah, I've had a great time, but I'll be glad to get home. You sure taught me a lot about trapping. Now I just have to practice."

"You're doing fine. I'll split the pay with you when I get paid."

"You keep the money. That's your pay for giving me trapping lessons. You are a real pro."

"My pleasure. Come on, help me pack up these pelts and we'll head to Sandy Lake."

Raymond did most of the packing, and realized that Uncle was having a hard time harnessing up the dogs.

"You'd better see your doctor when you get home," Raymond encouraged.

"I don't have anything wrong with me that a little beaver tail won't fix. Oh, by the way, here is a little beaver tail for your kohkom."

"Thanks," Raymond called after Uncle Henry who was hanging onto the sled, nearly losing control, as the three sled dogs headed for home.

"Hike!" Raymond yelled as he opened the throttle on the snowmobile. "Goodbye trap line."

• • •

204
201

CHAPTER 12

One day before present

The pleasant spring breeze rustled the bulging buds on the aspen trees as it ushered in the morning sunshine to warm up the Slave Lake Forestry Headquarters buildings nestled in a grove of trees bordering the Slave Lake airport. Across the parking lot stood the large warehouse, used to store the tons of equipment needed to fight forest fires in northern Alberta. Farther along the runway, large propeller driven airliners, called airtankers were being filled with chemical retardant from tall, reddish orange tanks.

"What kinds of airplanes are these?" Tim, the local newspaper reporter asked.

Tim was a young, energetic journalist, hoping to impress his demanding editor with a story that would catch the imagination of his readers, ensure him a permanent position as a writer for the local paper and maybe a promotion to a larger publication in the city.

"We have several planes working here now, but we may get more if the fire hazard becomes extreme," said Mel, the Information Officer assigned to show the reporter around.

Mel was a handsome, well groomed officer who had training in many aspects of the Forest Service. Because of his over-all knowledge of the Forest Service and his training in public relations, Mel made an ideal Information Officer. His good looks and charming manner were a bonus.

"The large white one with red and black stripes and a red tipped tail being filled at the tanks, is a Convair CV 580," Mel continued. "The CV 580 is a twin turbine engine airtanker built as an airliner, but now adapted with a big tank on the belly to convert it into an airtanker. The white one with a broad yellow stripe along each side, a yellow front and a black nose, is an Airspray Lockheed Electra or L-188 designed with constant flow tanks that can carry 3000 gallons of retardant."

"What about those yellow planes behind the red tanks?"

"The CL-215 is an amphibious flying boat-type aircraft specifically designed as a skimmer airtanker with the capacity of scooping water from a lake and delivering a mixture of water and foam to a fire. These are the yellow ones with red designs on the body and tail. They have the wings and two propeller engines attached on the top of the body."

"What are those funny looking planes that look like they have a crop sprayer on top of floats?"

"They are the newest airtankers of Alberta's Provincial fleet. They are the amphibious 802F Air Tractors."

"I see other smaller planes parked over here. What are they used for?"

"Each group of airtankers is required to be escorted by a smaller lead plane called a "birddog". They carry an Air Attack Officer (AAO) as well as the pilot. The white one with red stripes and twin propeller engines overhead is the Turbo Commander TC 690/A, used with the CV 580s and L-188s. The red and white one with curvy black lines and a single propeller engine in front is a Cessna Caravan C208 used with the CL-215s and Air Tractors."

"I've seen pictures with red retardant coming out of the water bombers. What is that?" Tim asked.

"There are two types of material used," Mel continued. "Foam is a white, aerated solution of water and an additive that helps to soak the fuel of a fire and extinguish flames. It is usually applied by the amphibious airtankers directly onto the flames. Foam and water are sometimes called suppressants. Long term fire retardants, like the pink one carried by the CV 580s, contain types of salts that slow down the change of solid wood to gas. Wood doesn't burn. It is the gas given off from the hot wood that ignites and burns."

"That is interesting. Wood doesn't burn."

"One kind of retardant is Phos-check 95A. It actually fertilizes the forest and helps it green up after the fire."

"How do they know where to drop the stuff?"

"The AAO has equipment that helps him locate hotspots, even in heavy smoke. He also gets information and directions from the Incident Commander, the

Area Duty Officer and the ground forces working on the fire. Then the birddog flies ahead of the airtanker, giving directions where and when the pilot should drop his load."

"How do they know when a fire starts?"

"Come," Mel said. "I'll show you the Wildfire Operations Office (WOO)."

The calm scene around the headquarters and the serene atmosphere of the open reception area belayed the somewhat frenzied, but deliberate, activity taking place behind the scene, in the various offices and in the Wildfire and Air Operations room. A large map of the Slave Lake district covered one wall. Different coloured pins identified the current fires.

Mel and Tim entered the room quietly making sure not to disturb Herb, the WOO Officer.

Herb was a middle-aged, barrel-chested officer, with a touch of gray showing around the temples. When it came to fighting forest fires, he sat next to God, having ultimate control over the activities in the district. His even tempered disposition and his steady voice did not flaunt the power he possessed. As a twenty plus year veteran of the Forest Service, he had progressed through the ranks to this position, struggling through the many changes and revisions of the Alberta Forest Service. His knowledge, perseverance and exceptional character earned him the respect of his superiors and the officers to whom he gave directions.

Herb was busy gathering information on the different fires in the district and planning strategy for getting everything under control. He was also giving directions to the Incident Commanders and the AAOs operating in the field. Sometimes, he needed to make forays into the field to get a firsthand look at fires from a helicopter.

The dispatch room, with its numerous modern wireless technologies, was bombarded with messages from the many lookout towers, the various aircraft and the Incident Commanders directing the current fire operations. Computer screens projected various sets of information including the latest weather forecast. Regular weather reports came in at 1030 and 1530. Fire tower weather was sent to Edmonton at 0740 and 1305. Weather briefings were made periodically and the results posted outside the dispatch room.

"The lookouts in their cupolas atop the various lookout towers in the district observe and report sightings of any smoke in their jurisdiction. The Wildfire Dispatcher is responsible for coordinating all of the communications coming into and going out of this office," Mel whispered, as he waved to Joyce one of the dispatchers. Her worried face masked her natural beauty.

Ted, the Duty Officer, stopped as Mel and Tim were looking at the weather notice.

"It doesn't look good," he said. "Hot, windy, and low humidity. The Fire Weather Index is getting pretty high. It looks like we have a number of holdover fires from that big lightning storm that went over the Marten Hills last week. That adds to the fires up North that are already out of control."

Ted was a rather short, rumpled type of guy, not fitting the typical description of a forest officer, but, in spite of his random abstract style and the snarl of papers on his desk, he had an exceptional ability to take full command of every aspect of his responsibilities.

"Thanks," Mel said, as Ted waved goodbye.

"How do they know what fires to fight first?" Tim asked Mel.

"As soon as a smoke is reported, a helitack crew, with a water bucket for the helicopter and an air tanker group are dispatched to the fire. The Duty Officer (DO) looks after the dispatches."

"How do they know who does what?" Tim asked as he continued his interview.

"There is a definite chain of command established by Sustainable Resource Development. It is called the Incident Command System (ICS). Herb puts various teams in place, with an officer in charge and then monitors the whole operation. Orders are given and others respond according to their position along the chain of command."

"What are the priorities, since there are a lot of fires going at once?"

"Well, they try to catch every fire with an initial attack crew, because it is better to put out a fire before it gets out of control. The first priority is human life in the settlements, next the property and then the areas near prime timber. After the initial attack crew starts to control the fire, various wildfire crews, including the ground crews with dozers and skidders go to work making fire guards and mopping up where the fire has gone through."

"We're taking a helicopter up North to check on the situation in the Wabasca and Sandy Lake region. The Sandy lookout sounded pretty worried," Herb announced.

A helicopter lifted smoothly into the air and headed north over the tree tops, with the rhythmic wop wop

wop and whirring of the blades echoing from the trees and the headquarter buildings.

"What kind of helicopter was that?" Tim asked.

"It was a Bell 206, four passenger with large blades, on top and small rotors on the tail. We have different rotary winged aircraft. The one sitting on the pad is the Astar, short for the Aerospatiale. It can carry a crew of five," Mel explained.

Just then, a mighty roar bellowed in from the runway, making it hard to talk. One of the CL-215's was taking off. Next a CV 580 started taxiing to the end of the runway, its propellers spinning with a high pitched whine.

"That's the big work horse," Mel yelled to Tim who was straining to hear above the cacophony of sound. Pointing to a huge helicopter, Mel yelled, "It is a Bell 212 that can carry a wildfire crew of eight men."

"I've had enough," Tim yelled, as he covered his ears. The big helicopter had fired up its engine and the blades started to spin.

"Did this help out with your story?" Mel yelled to Tim.

"Yes, but I'll put Joyce's picture on the front page. She's a lot better looking than you," Tim answered with a smile.

"Thanks a lot."

They waved goodbye.

The airport was coming alive. Air tankers, with their bird dog planes, were taking to the air, giving a thunderous roar that shook the ground and sent vibrations through anyone who might be standing at the airport. The pilots were enjoying the action. Technicians at the bomber base were filling another

CV 580 and checking to make sure they had sufficient material for the afternoon rush, which was sure to come. The whoomph, whoomph, pump, pump, pump sound of the big Bell helicopter, shattered the relative calm of the town as it lifted from the ground and headed north. A layer of smoke was hanging in the atmosphere and the morning sun was casting an eerie glow across the sky. The distinct smell of forest fire smoke filled the air around Slave Lake, as it drifted in from the north.

Suddenly, the radios came alive with a new message from the Sandy tower. "We have a new smoke up here."

• • •

CHAPTER 13

"Hi Joyce. We're on the ground at the Sandy Lake fire and it doesn't look good. We have a strong SE wind and we're losing control. We need some help," Julien reported.

Julien was the Helitack Leader of the crew at the Sandy Lake fire. He could hold a variety of positions because of his ten years of training and experience. He was a physically fit, high spirited man and loved the adrenalin rush of leading a helitack crew into a new fire and meeting the challenge of putting it out before it got out of control. His record was very good, but he was worried about this fire.

Julien and his highly trained crew had been dropped off on a hover exit. This was a rather risky maneuver, but necessary because of the uncertain landing terrain. The helicopter hovered over a small clearing, spotted with hummocks of grass sticking up. Two of the three man crew had to climb out onto the skids and lower themselves and their equipment into the unfamiliar muskeg. One got wet immediately.

The other one slipped into muddy gumbo while trying to unload his equipment. They started to clear a helicopter pad close to where the fire had gone through. Julien stayed with the helicopter until they found a better landing site from which to hook the water bucket onto the underside of the helicopter. He then helped the others to clear the pad and to start fighting the fire.

The water bucket, called a Bambi bucket was a large, collapsible water container that was suspended from a long cable hooked to the underside of the helicopter. As the helicopter lifted off from the ground, the cable stretched tightly and slowly pulled the container into the air. At a lake or stream near the fire, it was lowered and filled with water. The helicopter would then fly over the fire and at the appropriate place, the bottom was triggered to open and the water splashed down onto the fire.

"Art, we need a drop on the north side. It's getting pretty hot over there. We'll pull back and let you hit it," Julien advised over his radio.

Art was the Air Attack Officer in the birddog plane with the airtanker group of three CL-215s that had just arrived on the scene. Art and Julien, who was now considered the Incident Commander, were similar in age and physical build, but Art loved to fly and he relished flying with the birddog pilots. His three small children kept him entertained when he was not flying. His oldest boy was already a good hockey player.

Art and Julien were directing the efforts of the ground crew, the airtanker crew and the helicopter with the water bucket. This could be dangerous and careful coordination was needed so the aircraft did

not interfere with each other and crash. The ground crew had backpack type water bags called Wajax bags. With Wajax hand pumps, they tried to put out the ground fire. A horizontal bladed axe, called a Pulaski, was used to grub out the smoldering roots and moss. Once a drop was made the crew could establish an anchor point which would be safe and could serve as a base of operation for the fire.

"This is Kirk from Wabasca. We're sending in Harold and his dozer crew to give you guys ground support," Kirk radioed Julien. "Ted is looking for another bomber crew, but things are tight with all these fires going on up North."

"Thanks. We need a Convair in here and another group of Ducks. Sandy Lake is getting rough, but it is still calm enough by the river for the skimmers."

"Even if he finds another crew, remember, it will take an hour or so before they can get to Sandy"

"That may be too late."

Kirk was the Incident Commander in charge of the Wabasca district fires and he was located at the fire base there. He was a twelve year veteran of the Forest Service, having taken his training in Alberta and progressed through the ranks. He was a rugged type guy, who had started out as a city boy interested in a career in forestry. Soon, his leadership qualities were recognized as he moved through the ranks and he became a confident leader in his position as IC. His experience with major forest fires across Alberta and Canada helped him gain the respect of the men under his leadership.

Wabasca was a primary staging camp with two younger rangers and twenty-five additional firefighters who came to camp on a shift basis. Accommodation was available in mobile bunk houses, with a kitchen and washrooms serving the camp. There were radio, telephone, computer and fax communications on site. Wabasca was also a helibase where helicopters obtained fuel and the pilots could get their required amount of rest and enjoy the comforts of a motel until they were called into action.

Julien had hopped into a helicopter to help him spot an access route for the ground crew. He directed Harold, the Dozer Boss to bring in the heavy equipment along an abandoned and overgrown cut line. It was Harold's job to direct and to coordinate the movements of the D6 wide pads, D7 longs tracks, skidders with water tanks and pumps and the Nodwells and Bombardiers with water tanks and other fire fighting equipment. If the brush was not too thick, he could use a quad (ATV) to scout out the route ahead of the dozers.

Harold lived near Sandy Lake and he had a contracting business, using his heavy equipment in the oil patch and forest industry. He was now being contracted by the Forest Service to help fight the Sandy Lake fire. Harold started out as a dozer driver and he was now operating his own business with various types of equipment and several employees. His common sense approach to problems and his sense of humour, helped to make him a successful businessman and employer. The Forest Service knew they could count on Harold to do a superb job. His experience and advice were invaluable in fighting any forest fire.

"Hi, Julien. You guys can pull back a bit now. We'll make a fire guard and you can work with us," Harold announced over his radio.

"Okay. I can see a dozer now. Thanks."

The equipment was soon working along the flanks of the fire, taking away the fuel and directing the fire onto itself to eventually contain the fire and keep it from spreading. Another crew of eight fire fighters had arrived by helicopter. Many of them were locally trained Aboriginal men and women. They followed the equipment and put out fires along the way. The helicopter with the bucket worked in coordination with the tanker crew to hit the hot spots. An extra tanker crew arrived to help knock down the fire.

Overnight, the fire had died down because of the cooler temperatures, higher humidity and less wind.

"We should have this fire held until morning," Julien reported to Kirk.

"Okay."

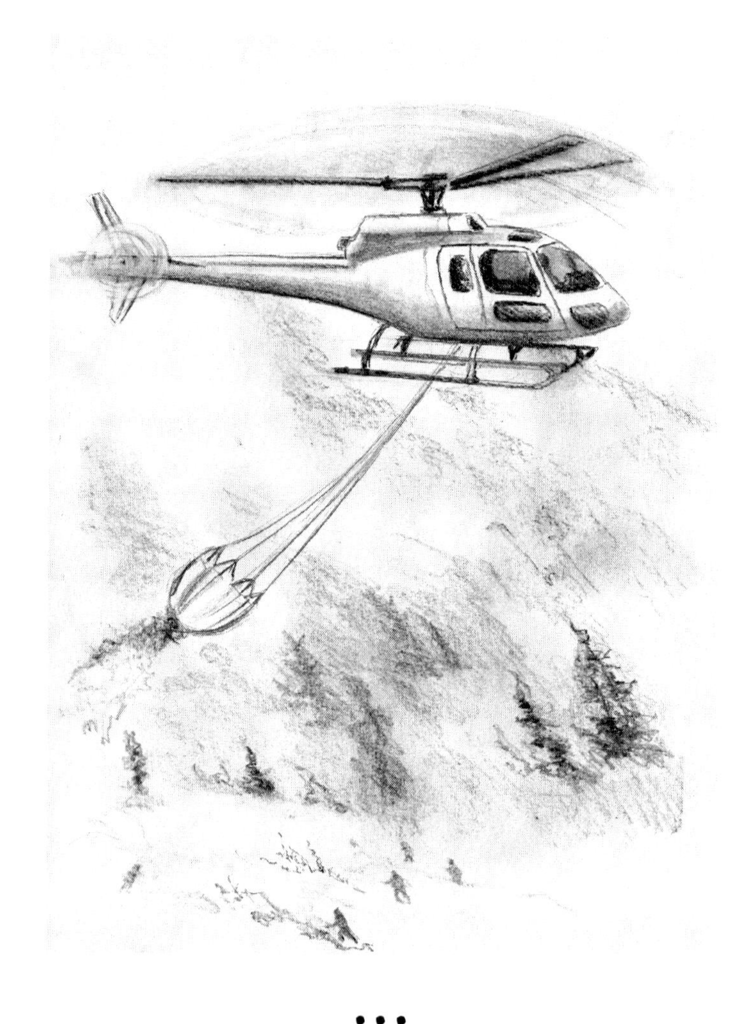

• • •

CHAPTER 14

Present time

An ominous pall of smoke hung over the Sandy Lake fire. The weather report this morning predicted high temperature and strong winds for the afternoon. The Fire Weather Index (FWI) was extreme. Kirk talked to the Wabasca logistics officer requesting more helicopters in case the Sandy Lake fire took off under the extreme conditions of the afternoon. The officer said Ted was looking for more helicopters for the helibase, but was having trouble finding fire fighting crews that weren't already committed to other fires. He knew he would need more men and equipment for a busy afternoon at Sandy Lake.

The bright sun glowed red, as its fiery rays beamed through the smoke that started to billow as the wind fanned the flames of the fire. A fire that was being held last night was soon whipped into a fully involved fire and threatening to break loose.

On the ground, Harold was getting his equipment operators to widen the fire guard and the ground crew was working hard to contain the fire. In the air, the helicopter with the bucket was making trip after trip, trying to control the hot spots, but it was difficult with the covering of smoke. The airtankers were also hampered by the thick layer of smoke. Soon, the fingers of the fire were shooting flames into the air. The flames and wind cleared the smoke, but this caused the various fingers of the fire to join together and before long the forest erupted into a blinding searing fire, like that of a monstrous blast furnace.

"Ted, we need help at Sandy Lake," Kirk announced.

"We're bringing in a bomber crew from Lac La Biche," Ted replied to all who were listening. "We're on Red alert."

From a helicopter high above, Julien announced, "Harold, pull out now! There is a lot of mature black spruce in there with no anchor points to work from and this fire could candle at any time."

When a ground fire started burning up the trunks of the trees, reaching the crowns, it was called candling. When the fire leapt from the crown of one tree to the crowns of other trees, it was said to be crowning.

"We're packing up. We did what we could with the fire guard, but it will jump any time now," Harold reported. We'll move to the safety zone with the others.

"Okay. Get everybody out," Herb confirmed the decision. "Start heading your crew toward the Town of Sandy Lake."

After consulting with Julien, Kirk and Harold, Herb said, "Kirk, I want you to be the IC for the Sandy Lake fire. Set up a base camp in the gravel pit near Sandy

Lake. We'll move in a camp from Slave Lake. We have another group of CL-215s on their way from Lac La Biche. Julien, you keep working with your crew."

Kirk put his assistant in charge of the Wabasca camp and he headed for the operation at Sandy Lake. Mobile units and equipment started rolling into the gravel pit near Sandy. Elmer, an elder from the local band office, was the Camp Officer for the Sandy Lake fire. He was giving directions to the truck drivers and the ground crew arriving to assemble the camp. The Sandy base camp would have a kitchen, washrooms, and tents to house and feed the fire crew. A temporary helibase was being set up with various helicopters coming and going.

"We need the oil and gas people to shut down their well sites east of Sandy Lake," Kirk directed from his helicopter. "Harold, I can see a cut line east of the Town of Sandy Lake. Get your crew in there and make a guard for the town."

"We have some fire injuries here," Julien reported. "We need an Ambulance Service."

"They'll have to come from Slave Lake because Wabasca is already dealing with another fire," Kirk responded.

"Did you get that, Ted?"

"Yes."

• • •

"The Sandy Lake fire just broke through the fire guard and it is now crowning in the black spruce. It's headed for the town," Art's voice echoed through the communication systems.

"Contact the MD (Municipal District) and the RCMP (Royal Canadian Mounted Police) to put the town on standby for possible evacuation," Kirk announced. Find some buses to use if we need to get everyone to Wabasca in a hurry. Ted, get a helicopter to bring some medical people in here right away. We may have a disaster brewing."

"Okay."

"We're having trouble making a fire guard around Sandy," Harold reported. "There's a lot of black spruce and muskeg. The equipment is sinking. This stuff will torch like kindling when the fire hits it."

"Be ready to pull out," Kirk advised.

• • •

CHAPTER 15

Radios and telephones crackled alive with the voice of the IC.

"Sandy Lake needs to be evacuated now!" Kirk announced. We may not have a lot of time. This fire is an inferno and a southerly is bringing a wall of fire toward the town."

"We lost the fire guard," another voice broke into Kirk's announcement. "We got the operators out, but some of the equipment is burning."

"Okay, put all remaining equipment and manpower to Sandy Lake town as soon as possible," Kirk radioed from his helicopter high above the fire. "I want everyone to concentrate on the east side. We'll help evacuate the people, and try to save the town. Are there enough buses for those that don't have a ride? We need some for the crews in case we have to abandon the town."

"This is the fire department from Slave Lake. We're on our way with the fire and rescue unit. Do you still want us to come to Sandy?" a voice asked.

"Yes. Our base camp is at the gravel pit and at this point, it is safe. You can set up there."

"We have a burn casualty who should be flown out," someone reported. "Is there a helicopter available?"

"There will be emergency services at the Sandy Base. Get your patient there, first, and a chopper will be waiting."

"Okay, I'll check."

"Bad news," Kirk announced over the radio. "The Sandy fire has split and is spreading to the north side of the lake. Does anyone know what it's like over there? It looks like mostly black spruce and muskeg from the helicopter. Are those timber resources committed?"

"There are no industries operating over there," a voice responded. "Muskeg and black spruce, that's all."

"Okay. We'll concentrate on the town and leave the north side for now."

"Hey, Kirk, we've got a guy at Sandy who says he's not leaving. He says he's got family living on a trap line on the north side of the lake and won't leave without them."

"I'll swing around there and check it out," Herb said from his helicopter high in the sky where he was monitoring the action. "Kirk, you concentrate on the town."

• • •

"Sylvia!" Raymond called.

"Sylvia!" Arlene called.

"You check by the lake," Raymond called to Arlene. "I'll check by the dogs."

Sylvia loved water. She loved to slap her hands on the surface of the lake and to splatter water all over herself and anyone who happened to be close by. She was not allowed to go down to the dog kennels, but she loved the dogs and she may have wandered down there to try to pet the dogs.

Arlene ran to the lake, calling for Sylvia. A hint of panic was in her voice. She ran past the boat that had a new coat of fiberglass and paint, down past the canoe, used so many times to get away from the stresses of family life and to enjoy the serenity of the lake. Now, the lake that held so many pleasant experiences seemed to be embroiled in a catastrophe. The calm of the morning was replaced by pounding waves and pounding hearts.

Raymond ran to the kennels calling "Sylvia! Sylvia-a-a-a!"

He ran down past the smoky, tanning fire, past the smoke house and the log ice house, with its chunks of ice, cut from the lake last winter and now covered with sawdust, shavings and hay, ready to keep things frozen for most of the summer. The dogs started their chorus of barking and snarling, thinking they were going to get fed. Sylvia was nowhere to be found.

"Sylvia!" Raymond called as he ran on down to the nearby creek. Maybe Sylvia was attracted by the icy cold water and she was dabbling her feet in it. No Sylvia.

"Where can she be? We've looked everywhere."

Raymond ran back along the creek to the lake and he met Arlene coming his way.

"Nothing?"

"Nothing."

Arlene was in tears and the knot in Raymond's gut was starting to tighten as if it were being squeezed in a vice.

"Maybe by the new cabin!" Raymond called, as he ran to the partially constructed log cabin. "You check again, around the ice house."

The new cabin was the dream home of the young couple who had decided to come north to live by the old ways. It was taking a lot of time and effort and there didn't seem to be enough time to work on it. They had cut and transported the logs, peeled and dried them, but it was hard work to cut, to notch and to put the logs into place. The dream would be nothing without Sylvia.

"Sylvia!" No answer.

"Arlene!" Raymond called, as he ran around the edge of the ice house. Arlene had collapsed in a sobbing ball of frustration.

"She's not here!" she screamed.

"It's all my fault," Raymond castigated himself as he threw his arms around Arlene. "I didn't watch her closely enough."

Raymond held Arlene in an excruciating huddle, amid sobs and gut wrenching bursts of pain. Their little girl Sylvia was missing. They had looked everywhere and they couldn't find her. There was no trace or clue where she might be. Gale force winds were thrashing the trees and blowing dust and debris into ugly looking swirls like miniature tornadoes. Dark clouds of rain and smoke were billowing in the east.

"Arlene," Raymond said, "I think the tanning fire is putting out sparks and it is starting little fires in the dry grass. I have to try to put them out."

Raymond ran to the shed for a shovel and he started covering the tanning fire with dirt. He also tried to cover the spot fires that were spreading around him.

Then the panic attack hit. The small fires were erupting into blazing fires and heading toward the cabin.

"Arlene!" Raymond yelled. "Run to the emergency radio by the truck and call for help!"

Raymond had a short wave radio, stored in his rust bucket of a truck and he could plug it into the truck battery to use in emergencies. The truck was parked across the creek next to an old logging trail. A makeshift log bridge was the only way to get to the truck.

"Be careful on the bridge," Raymond warned. "Attach the battery cables and call Wabasca."

"I forget how!" Arlene yelled back.

"The instructions are on the side of the radio. I'm going to the lake for water."

Raymond grabbed a couple of buckets and he ran along the path to the lake.

"Sylvia!" he called as he ran.

No Sylvia.

Raymond scooped up the water and turned to run up the bank. Across the lake, he could see the billowing of the smoke mixed with the storm clouds. Heat from the fire forced smoke and clouds into surging plumes of varying colours, ranging from white to ominous blue and black. Raymond also noticed the telltale colour of black spruce smoke coming from the southeast part of Sandy Lake. The fire could come through the muskeg on the north side of the lake. If it were a crowning fire, the extreme heat would cause the needles on the spruce trees to burst into a flaming blaze even before the main ground fire arrived. Raymond didn't know how much time they had, but he knew he had to get help, and in the mean time he would soak down the cabin and surrounding area.

"Sylvia!" Raymond called as he ran with the heavy buckets of water, sloshing it over the sides. The buckets were crashing into his flailing legs as he tripped on the debris, now littering the trail as a result of the blustering wind.

No Sylvia.

Raymond grabbed some spare burlap bags, used to store ice in the ice house, and he soaked them in the water. He started using them to beat out the fire that was spreading into the grass. He leaned a makeshift ladder against the cabin and climbed up to pour water along the peak of the roof, hoping it would prevent sparks from catching the roof on fire. He ran for more water, desperate to prepare their cabin for the fire that was imminent.

"Sylvia!"

No Sylvia.

On the return trip, Raymond saw Arlene, water soaked and blood spotted. She screamed at Raymond as she slumped near the smoke house.

"Help me!"

"What happened?

"I slipped on the bridge and skinned my arms and legs when I fell into the water."

"Here, put the wet bag on your cuts and push tight to stop the bleeding." Even in the midst of all the water, blood, and tears, Raymond noticed this lovely woman. He loved her dearly, and he regretted having brought her here to endure such pain.

"Did you call Wabasca?"

"No, I couldn't get it to work," Arlene said as she lay sobbing on the ground.

"Here," Raymond said putting the water bucket next to her, "when you can, soak the bag and swing it onto the ground to put out the grass fire."

Raymond started running toward the bridge and the truck.

"Sylvia!"

No Sylvia.

Raymond panted, as he grabbed the wires to the radio. He plugged them in. No radio.

"What's wrong? Maybe corrosion."

Raymond checked the wires on the truck battery and scraped off some of the corrosion. The radio came alive with a burst of sound.

"Yes!"

Raymond turned the dial.

"Static!"

Raymond worked frantically turning the dial back and forth searching for any contact. He tried every possible setting, and every other frequency, trying to get help. He got only static. Then Raymond realized that he and Arlene were facing a raging forest fire alone.

"No!"

"Sylvia!" Raymond called, as he ran for the bridge and the cabin to continue carrying water and fighting the grass fire that was gaining momentum.

No Sylvia.

The dogs were howling and putting up a big fuss as Raymond ran past.

"Shadow!" Raymond said as he stopped and turned back to the kennels.

Going back to Shadow, Raymond talked gently to the dog as he untied his chain.

"Shadow. Find Sylvia. Keep her safe and bring her back."

Raymond untied the other dogs and they ran for the creek.

Shadow loped East in the direction of the fire.
"Sylvia-a-a-a!"
No Sylvia.

• • •

CHAPTER 16

"We have a couple over here by a little cabin trying to beat out some grass fires," Herb announced. He had put a deputy in charge for an hour and had come north to check out the Sandy Fire. "They may not realize that the big one is headed their way. Kirk, you'll need a helitack crew over here on the north side of the lake. Bring a pump and a sprinkler system. We might be able to help them save their cabin. That wind is whipping pretty good over here and the fire is crowning through the black spruce. I can tell from the black, bronzy smoke it's a rank six crown fire. The way it is going now we don't have a lot of time before the fire is at the cabin. Is there any equipment on the north side of the lake? We need a fire guard."

There was no response from Kirk whose helicopter was on the pad at Sandy getting fuel.

"We have to return to Slave Lake," the pilot announced as he swung the helicopter around the site with a low, sweeping maneuver. The treetops seemed to swirl under their feet as the branches passed under the bubble of glass enclosing the cabin. "We're maxed out on our allowed air time and we need some maintenance as well."

"Okay," Herb agreed, speaking into the microphone attached to his headset. Headsets with microphones were necessary to allow the occupants in the cabin of the helicopter to hear each other above the loud, whirring vibration of the spinning blades overhead.

"I hate to leave these guys on their own. I'll try to get help for them as soon as I can. They have no idea what is coming at them. Did you see any spots where you could land a helicopter?"

"It looked as if there was an old well site near where the truck was sitting. That could work in an emergency, but this wind would make it pretty tricky."

"We could bring in a float plane, but that lake looks mighty rough. I did see a big fishing boat struggling through the waves. They might be able to help."

"Why don't you call again," the pilot's voice buzzed through the headphones.

"Okay." Herb repeated the call.

"This is Casey," a husky sounding voice boomed into the radio. "I've put the call out for more equipment, but there doesn't seem to be anyone on the north side of Sandy Lake. Everything is at the town site and a dozer group is at the Prairie, east of Sandy clearing a guard for the ranch. They're worried the fire will come through there."

Casey was the Fire Chief for Sandy Lake. He was a respected and long time resident. In fact he was born at Sandy and he had gone to school in the one room school house with one teacher. This giant of an Aboriginal man could organize anything and he was now trying to ensure the safety of the residents and their property.

"Thanks, Casey. Ted, we're coming in for maintenance. See if there are any spare helicopters and air tankers in northern Alberta. We have some people on the north side of Sandy Lake and we're going to have to get them out in the next two to three hours. We have fire all around the east side of the lake now."

"I'll see what I can do," Ted responded. "You're sure making headlines up there. The news people want to have a look at the fire. The call for the evacuation of Sandy Lake triggered a frenzy from the media."

"Hold them off and whatever you do, don't mention that there are people trapped on the north shore."

"Got it."

• • •

Raymond and Arlene heard the helicopter go over and they hoped that someone would come to help them. They lost all hope when the aircraft circled and left them on their own.

"Sylvia!" Arlene called between swings of the water soaked burlap bags.

"Sylvia! Shadow!" Raymond called as he ran for more water.

Sometimes the wind changed direction and it seemed to die down. It gave them hope that the fire would change direction and turn away from the cabin. Then, suddenly, the force of the wind whipped up the fire and the smoke from the main fire spread its acrid, choking fumes over the small clearing in the forest.

The beautiful, picturesque landscape, that had held so much promise as the serene home of their dreams was now becoming a prison.

"If the fire comes through here, we'll have to make a run for the lake!" Raymond yelled to Arlene through the storm.

"I'm not leaving without Sylvia!" Arlene shouted back.

"That's a last resort, but we may have to."

"Sylvia!"

"Shadow!"

• • •

Coming into the Slave Lake airport, Herb noticed two more CV 580s loading up retardant at the bright reddish orange tanks. The helicopter touched down lightly on its refueling spot. The crew bent low under the spinning blades, following government safe exit procedures, and they hurried into headquarters to get the latest from the weather briefing. It wasn't good. The two additional CV 580s, with their birddog planes had just arrived from Whitecourt and the pilots listened to their instructions for the Sandy Lake fire. They were assigned to the north shore. Art would give them final instructions and direct all air traffic, making sure there were no conflicts in the flight patterns.

Just as they were leaving headquarters, the ground and everything on it shook in synchronization with the vibrations of a large Armed Forces helicopter as it landed. It had been diverted from a training flight in Cold Lake. The helicopter and its crew were ready to head to Sandy Lake. They loaded up additional men and supplies, including water pumps and sprinklers, and followed the directions to Sandy Lake.

"Hey, Herb," Kirk broke into the steady stream of radio messages. "We have a helicopter with a bucket coming from High Level. More heavy equipment is coming by road from Calling Lake. Another helitack crew is coming from Trout Lake. How much did you bribe these guys with anyway?" Kirk teased.

"You'll find out on your next pay check," Herb joked.

He felt a lot more like joking now than he did when returning to Slave Lake. Maybe there was hope for the couple on the north shore after all. He wished he could let them know that help was on the way.

"Is there any way to contact the couple on the north shore of Sandy?" Herb asked.

"Someone said they have an emergency radio, but reception is really bad over there."

"We're on our way over there now," Kirk reported. "Can anyone see the fire on the north shore?"

"Yeah," Art replied. "It doesn't look good. It is billowing pretty good and moving fast."

"How much time do we have?"

"Not much."

"Is the helitack crew there, yet?"

"Don and his crew just left Wabasca."

"Okay."

• • •

CHAPTER 17

"We're at the north shore cabin," Don, the young, but dedicated Helitack Leader reported. "The bucket is ready and the crew is working on clearing a landing pad. We're controlling the grass fires and putting a guard around the cabin site, but we've got a big problem. A little girl is missing in the bush. The parents are pretty worked up. Can we get a search and rescue team in here right away?"

"Okay."

"We'll have the landing pad ready."

"Okay. The RCMP has your message."

Immediately, orders started filtering down the chain of command. Police detachments in the surrounding areas were alerted. Officers were deployed. The Slave Lake Air/Ground Ambulance was already at Sandy Lake with an ambulance, but an air ambulance and crew were also dispatched. Ambulances from the MD and local reserves were notified. The Forest Service directed the fire control aspect of the emergency.

"Kirk, did you get that? We have a little girl missing at the Sandy Lake cabin," Herb announced. "We have to stop the north shore fire."

"Yes. We're already redirecting the Ducks."

The life of a lost girl took priority over the buildings at Sandy Lake. The town had been evacuated and the crew at the base camp was safe.

"Where did you see her last?" Don asked Raymond.

"Beside the moose hide," Raymond answered in a somber voice.

"What is her name?"

"Sylvia," Arlene nearly shouted. She had been yelling Sylvia for so long and her frustration nearly peaked when she told the officer. Her bank of tears was nearly dry from crying so much and her nerves were nearly shattered.

"Where have you looked so far?"

"We've looked all around the cabin and the lake front," Raymond informed Don.

"I checked by the creek, but there was no sign of her," Arlene stuttered out the words. "What are we going to do?" The bank of tears filled and overflowed again.

"There are a lot of game trails yet that we haven't followed. I don't know how she got away from us," Raymond mumbled. He still couldn't believe that Sylvia was gone but for the first time, he realized he was no longer in control. From here on he had to ride the tide.

"That's okay, help is on the way. We'll find her."

"But the fire," Arlene sobbed.

"Okay. Both of you, help us bring the hose from the lake and we'll get the sprinkler set up on the house." Don knew he had to put the couple to work or they might run off again down some game trail and then he would have three lost people.

His thoughts were soon drowned out by the rhythmic sound of a rotary wing beating the air as it landed on the makeshift landing pad. The crew ran for cover and it lifted off again, only to be replaced by other choppers bringing more people and equipment.

"Over here!" Marie yelled as she assembled the search crew.

Marie was a tall, matronly type woman who could command attention with just her voice. One could sense that inattention would bring swift action and it wouldn't be pleasant on the part of the receiver. Some of the people could envision a not-so-pleasant teacher from their past. In any case, Marie took charge of the search and she garnered respect, not just from her voice, but from her reputation as one of the most experienced search organizers in the province.

"Okay, here is the plan. Do exactly what I tell you or we'll have to come looking for you, as well as this sweetie of a three year old," Marie said with emphasis. Deep inside she knew this search was different than most. Even though the long days in the North Country would allow the search to continue until after 2200 hours, there was a time limit and the smoke and ash in the howling wind, punctuated this thought.

"Don, keep Raymond and Arlene busy at the cabin. Jenny, look after Arlene and don't let her out of your sight. We don't want her running off on her own."

Marie directed the search, Jenny, an Aboriginal EMT (Emergency Medical Technician) from Sandy Lake, kept an eye on Arlene. Don, Kirk and Art directed the fire fighting. They were hitting the fire with all of their resources, but the low humidity and wind in the black spruce forest type was hampering their efforts to control it. It was bearing down on the little cabin in spite of everything.

"We need enough helicopters to evacuate everyone in case we lose this one," Herb announced. "There is a landing space across the creek, west of the cabin. You can see the old truck there. Wait on the cutline."

"There's a fishing boat here at the cabin, as well. They said they'll stand by and can take on people if necessary," Kirk responded.

"Okay."

• • •

"Evacuate now!" the directive came over the communication network.

The raging fire was closing in on the cabin and putting the rescue operation in the direct line of its destructive path. The last resort was to abandon the girl, but they needed to save the lives of the rescuers and forestry workers. People hurriedly followed the path to the creek and on to the waiting helicopters. No one said a word. There was a warranted, despondent feeling creeping through the group. Some were in tears.

"We're not going!" Raymond yelled as he grabbed Arlene and they ran for the lake. "We won't leave our baby!"

"I'm staying with you!" Jenny called as she ran behind them.

Kirk and Don were close behind.

As Raymond and Arlene were plunging into the water, the fishing boat came in to meet them. Kirk, Don, Jenny and the two burly fishermen wrestled the yelling Raymond and the screaming Arlene into the boat. The boat gradually backed away from the shore.

Raymond and Arlene collapsed on the bottom of the boat, completely defeated and exhausted.

"Oh, God, save our baby!" Raymond called. His voice lost in the void of the pounding waves, or was it?

The helicopters lifted all of the people to safety beyond the fire. Everyone would be available to continue the search when it was again safe to return to the cabin.

• • •

CHAPTER 18

Amid the smoke and ash, Raymond could recognize the outline of the cabin, with a green perimeter around it, where the sprinklers had sprayed the water.

"I think the cabin's okay," Raymond spoke first.

"Is it possible that Sylvia survived the fire?" Arlene asked.

"Well," Kirk replied reservedly, sometimes the fire skips around depending on the wind and the forest type. It looks like the fire took the black spruce east and north of the cabin, but it skipped over the aspen by the cabin. There may be other spots where the fire skipped, but who knows?"

"You're clear to go back in to continue the search," Kirk announced. "The fire has cooled a bit and the smoke has lifted. Watch out for the hot spots. By the way, the Sandy Lake fire missed the town. This northern fire skipped over the cabin and there are a few other unburned spots. We'll continue hitting the fire from above, but I think it's turning away from the lake. We'll start mop up procedures around the cabin."

"Okay," Marie directed, "we'll continue our search. Check every unburned spot, but be safe. We still have some flames and smoke."

"Come on!" Raymond yelled to Arlene as soon as they could jump from the boat.

Arlene tried to follow, but Raymond was way ahead. Jenny was also following behind.

The fire had cleared out a lot of the underbrush and this had exposed game trails that Raymond never knew existed. Since Shadow had run toward the fire, Raymond had a premonition that Sylvia was east of the cabin. The cabin site was still in good condition and it would soon recover, but, now, he had to find Sylvia. Raymond skirted the flames still shooting up from the burning trees and the deadfall. Black, charred trees were everywhere and some burning branches came crashing down as he ran along the trails.

"Sylvia-a-a-a!" Raymond called.

"Sylvia-a-a-a!" Arlene called.

Raymond was frantically searching for Sylvia. Then the reality struck him squarely in the gut. He nearly fainted. This was not like searching for Sylvia before the fire went through. Raymond realized, for the first time, that even if he found Sylvia, she could be as charred as these stumps.

"Noooo!" Raymond screamed as he continued along a trail.

"What is that?"

Raymond recognized the sound of barking dogs in the distance.

"Dogs!" Raymond said as he stumbled in the direction of the barking sounds.

"Shadow!"

Raymond heard Shadow barking and snarling ferociously. Wait! This was not his Shadow. This was Mosôm's Shadow from the distant past. Another dog barked and snarled. Raymond recognized this sound from his encounter on Dog Island. This was the ferocious, black dog that had attacked him on the island.

"Shadow!" Raymond screamed as the dogs continued to fight and to bite each other. Then they tumbled down a bank, out of sight.

Raymond started to pursue the fighting dogs, but then he heard a soft bark and whine coming from a shallow slough with unburned clumps of grass, surrounded by water and nestled in an island of tamarack trees.

"Shadow! What are you doing here?" Raymond asked as he approached the husky, with now scorched and blackened hair.

Raymond was confused. This was his Shadow. Where did the other dogs go?

"Sylvia!" Raymond cried as he dropped to his knees, splashing them into the cold water. He had discovered the small bundle of a girl curled up on a clump of grass, sheltered from harm by his white husky, Shadow.

"Arlene!" Raymond called. "We found them, Sylvia and Shadow."

"Sylvia," was all Raymond could verbalize. Raymond huddled with both Sylvia and Shadow. They all seemed a bit dazed.

"Shadow and I were hiding," Sylvia said in an innocent voice. Shadow had protected her from the fire and he had kept her warm, but she still showed signs of fright and hypothermia.

Arlene ran up and joined the huddle. There were hugs and tears, enough for the whole rescue squad. Jenny and the others watched in awe.

"Thank God, you're safe," Arlene said as she kissed Sylvia. "Okay, you too," she said when Shadow nudged her.

"Thank you, everyone!" Raymond called out.

"Okay, bring Sylvia. We're getting all of you to Slave Lake. We want you three checked out by a doctor," Jenny told them. "Sorry, Shadow, not you."

"But, we're okay now!" Raymond objected. "Who'll look after the dogs?"

"Your friends in the boat said they'll look after your place until you get back tomorrow. Let's go while we still have some daylight," Marie ordered. Everyone agreed, even Raymond.

• • •

CHAPTER 19

Raymond felt so mixed up as he carried Sylvia and followed Arlene onto the big Bell 212 medivac helicopter. He was awestruck as they lifted off the ground, giving him an overview of the cabin, the burned out forest and the fire that was still burning, but being held for the night.

"Grandpa!" Raymond said to himself as he looked out over the vast forest. "You and Shadow were here. I know it, but I'll never be able to prove it." Raymond shook with grief and happiness. He realized that he had been searching for Grandpa all of these years, but Grandpa was always with him. Grandpa and the grandpas before him were all part of this land and its spirit. Raymond now knew he was part of that same land and spirit. His journey on the land would be different from any person before or after him. He was unique and he could be sure that the land and its spirit would be with him forever. Arlene and Sylvia were now woven into his being and they would travel with him wherever he went, during whatever challenges he faced. Raymond also realized that as much as he loved living by the old ways, his journey would take him out of the bush and back to Slave Lake. They needed to be with their families. Sylvia would need a good education and he and Arlene needed to associate with all kinds of people. They needed support from their immediate family to ensure the old ways were preserved, but he also realized how much they needed the non-Native people of the community. People of all nationalities, culture, colour, race and religion had sacrificed time and effort to save the cabin and to search for Sylvia. He couldn't thank them enough, but he now realized that he could contribute his time, his effort and his skills to help others in a community that had responded so quickly and graciously to help his family when they were in desperate need. Raymond knew that the land would recover, over time. It was the way things had happened in the forest for centuries. His people had lived with forest fires and survived. His trap line would recover. The cabin had survived. He could still come here at any time to work on the new cabin and enjoy some hunting and trapping, but for now he knew he had to go back to Slave Lake and begin the next chapter in his life. He smiled.

"Now I can be an Indian and a white man. Not like Mother who gave up the old ways, but I can have the best of both worlds. I can have a job as a mechanic, have both Indian and white friends and I know I can live by the old ways if I want to. This will be good for Sylvia and her family. Hey! Wait just a minute. I don't want to be a mosôm!"

• • •

Raymond and his family returned to the cabin the day after the fire.

"Hey, Arlene!" Raymond called. "This moose hide is already smoked. That was a pretty big smoking fire you made," Raymond teased. "Do you want to take the hide along out to Slave Lake?"

"Yes," Arlene replied from the cabin where she was keeping Sylvia behind doors. She was being a bit overprotective, but Sylvia was not going to run off again before they were back in Slave Lake.

Friends and relatives from both Sandy Lake and Slave Lake were helping Raymond and Arlene pack up and move back to Slave Lake. Raymond was trying to decide what to leave in case he would come back in the fall to do some hunting and trapping. Arlene was boxing everything.

"Hey, Arlene!" Raymond called, "leave a few things for when we come back hunting this fall."

"I'm not planning to come back here for a long time. Maybe, when Sylvia is a teenager."

"Ha, we'll see. You'll want to smoke another hide before that."

"Smoking is the man's job, remember?"

The humour was returning to the banter between Raymond and Arlene, but their lives and future had been changed forever by the forest fire.

"Don't forget to feed the dogs," Arlene called to Raymond, "or they'll be barking the whole way home."

"Don't forget to feed me or I'll be nagging you the whole way home," Raymond teased.

The cabin was closed up, but not locked, in case Uncle Henry or anyone else needed a place to stay on the trap line. The rust bucket of a truck was loaded, with the dogs in their boxes, everything was tied down and Arlene and Sylvia were buckled into the front seat with Raymond.

"Goodbye," they said to their friends.

"Goodbye."

Everyone traveled together on the cut line road out to Sandy Lake and then on to Slave Lake.

• • •

When they got to the Provincial Park, Raymond decided to take the beach road along the lake and to stop at Devonshire Beach before going home. A short distance up the road, they came upon a truck stopped by the side of the road and a guy had the hood up, looking at the engine.

"Need some help?" Raymond called out as he pulled his truck up behind. The dogs started barking and the guy looked a bit apprehensive as Raymond approached.

"I stopped to do a bit of bird watching along the lake and for some reason, the battery ran down. Now, I can't get it started."

"No problem," Raymond told him. "I have a set of jumper cables somewhere in this truck. Raymond checked behind the seat and he pulled out the cables with red and black ends.

"Put the red end on the positive post of your battery and the black on the negative post. I'll do the same on mine," Raymond said as he lifted his truck hood and attached the cables.

"Okay. Try starting your engine," Raymond instructed.

The engine fired up right away and the cables were removed and put away.

"Thank you so much. What do I owe you? It would have been a long walk into town."

"Nothing" Raymond replied. "Just return the favour to someone else who needs a helping hand. A lot of people helped me out recently and I'm more than happy to help you out."

'What do you do in Slave Lake?"

"Well, I'm a mechanic, but I've been living up North for awhile. We're moving back to Slave Lake."

"I thought I recognized you. You've worked on this truck once before."

"That's right. Now, I remember. We worked on the brakes."

"You're a good mechanic. Here, take this and get something for the family."

"Thank you," Raymond said as he took a folded bill.

"Thank you!"

Raymond continued along the beach road and he stopped the truck at one of the pullouts. Everybody had a chance to get out and to stretch. Arlene ran with Sylvia along the water's edge. Raymond stood on a bluff overlooking the lake and he focused on Dog Island.

"I'm home," Raymond thought. "This is where I belong. I know Mosôm is with me and we are all part of the circle of life." Raymond recalled the Elders teaching about the circle of life with its four directions. East was the beginning place with the rising sun representing insight and goal setting. South represented things of the heart, childlike innocence and trust. West represented the place of thoughts and introspection. North represented the place of wisdom and knowledge. Raymond, in the centre of the circle, needed to balance these directions and pursuits, including an open door for his ancestors, to maintain a well-rounded circle. He now realized the need to continue nurturing these principles within himself and his family. Raymond recalled the footsteps of his past, the progress he had made, the obstacles he had overcome, and he could look forward to the many good things to come. Raymond had not found Grandfather on Dog Island, but he had solved the mystery of Dog Island by participating in the ways of his grandfather and the many grandfathers before him.

"Sylvia!" Raymond called as he ran and jumped down the sand dune. He splashed into the lake beside Sylvia and Arlene, spraying them with the cold water. Raymond was glad to be home and so were Arlene and Sylvia. Raymond gathered up one girl in each arm and he swung them around with his bulging muscles. Everyone was having a great time.

"We're going to have a baby," Arlene whispered into Raymond's ear.

"What!"

"We're going to have a baby boy."

"How do you know that?"

"Ancient kohkom secret."

"Get real!"

"I am!"

"Okay, okay. If it is going to be a boy, can we name him Alphonse, after Mosôm?"

"Sure."

"Alright," Raymond said. I guess its all part of the circle of life."

"What are you talking about?"

"I'll tell you some time," Raymond said as he grabbed Sylvia and ran up the dune to the truck.

"Wait for me."

"Come on. Let's see if Kohkom has some moose meat and bannock. I'm hungry."

• • •